Beneath the streetlights,

he watched shadows dance across her features. His gaze went to her lips. "Did you know that there are a lot of lost arts?"

"Really," Meg answered, starting to draw away, but he held firm. "Like what?"

"Spooning." He grinned as he used the antiquated term.

His answer threw her off-balance. An amused smile tugged at the corners of her lips. "Spooning?"

"Uh-huh." Briefly, his gaze returned to hers and then drifted back to her mouth. "No one takes the time for it anymore. Today, it's a look across a room, your place or mine, and bed. No time for... kissing, caressing, loving," he finished on a whisper. "Seems a shame, doesn't it? That something that enjoyable is being forgotten."

She anticipated his kiss. She wanted it, she realized, tilting her head slightly.

Then his mouth met hers.

Dear Reader,

Welcome to Silhouette. Experience the magic of the wonderful world where two people fall in love. Meet heroines who will make you cheer for their happiness, and heroes (be they the boy next door or a handsome, mysterious stranger) who will win your heart. Silhouette Romances reflect the magic of love—sweeping you away with books that will make you laugh and cry, heartwarming, poignant stories that will move you time and time again.

In the next few months, we're publishing romances by many of your all-time favorites, such as Diana Palmer, Brittany Young, Emilie Richards and Arlene James. Your response to these authors and other authors of Silhouette Romances has served as a touchstone for us, and we're pleased to bring you more books with Silhouette's distinctive medley of charm, wit and—above all—*romance*.

I hope you enjoy this book and the many stories to come. Experience the magic!

Sincerely,

Tara Hughes
Senior Editor
Silhouette Books

Books by Jennifer Mikels

Silhouette Special Edition

A Sporting Affair #66
Whirlwind #124

Silhouette Romance

Lady of the West #462
Maverick #487
Perfect Partners #511

JENNIFER MIKELS

uses her extensive travel experience as research for her writing. She's ventured all over the East Coast, Canada, and practically every northern state and loved every minute of it. Her home base is Phoenix, Arizona, where she lives with her husband and two sons, where they share a love of the West, the country and mountain camping.

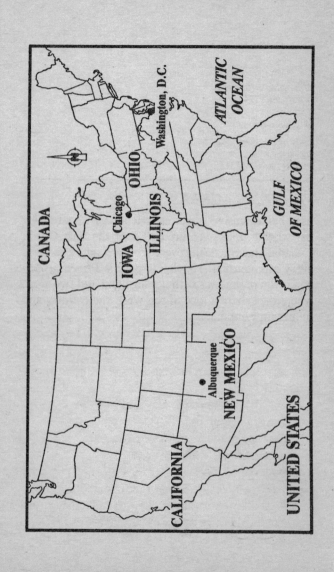

Prologue

Are you giving the nurses a hard time?" Ryan Brady mumbled into the telephone receiver as he stretched the cord around the stove so he could reach the refrigerator.

James Gallagher shifted the phone to a more comfortable position against his ear, wondering if his friend realized what time it was. The clock on the table beside him showed seven in the morning. "What time is it in Albuquerque?"

"Six," Ryan answered, reaching into the refrigerator for a jar of mayonnaise.

"It's seven in the morning in Chicago."

Ryan grimaced. "Woke you, huh?"

Humor edged Jim's voice. "Not any more than these nurses have, pestering me with their thermometers."

"No good-looking nurses," Ryan deducted, knowing that Jim wouldn't be complaining if there were.

"Not that I've seen."

"Well, I'm returning the call you left on my answering machine."

"That was two days ago. Where have you been for the past few days?"

"On a stakeout." Ryan piled two more slices of turkey on top of a slice of bread. "For the last thirty-six hours."

"You cops have a hard life."

"I wouldn't mind if we'd been able to book the guy. But someone forgot to read him his rights."

"Sounds as if you're getting tired of the red tape."

Ryan snapped open a can of beer and took a hearty swallow before answering, "Could be."

"Are you thinking about that partnership with me?"

"Could be."

Jim laughed. "Sometimes you're annoying."

Ryan smiled and added another slice of ham to his inch-high creation. "Since you're obviously at a disadvantage, I'll let that pass."

"I am down," Jim said lightly, enjoying his own pun. "Flat on my back with a cast on my leg."

"You never told me how that happened."

"Why don't we forget it?"

"Come on," Ryan insisted, guessing that if Jim wasn't talking, the incident had to be embarrassing.

"I'll tell you later. The details aren't important. I called you before because I have a favor to ask," Jim said seriously. "Could you get away? And would you be willing to come here?"

Ryan frowned at the receiver in his hand. "You want me to come to Chicago?"

"Yeah. I started another case on the day that I broke my leg. The woman who hired me could be in danger. Some guy is harassing her."

Ryan took a large bite of the sandwich while he considered the favor. He'd been thinking more and more about Jim's proposal that they form a partnership. The idea of being his own boss appealed to him. He also was getting tired of the strict regimentation that he felt on the police force. Even the thought of moving held an appeal. Though he liked the Southwest, he'd lived in Washington a few years before and had liked living in the big city. Jim's suggestion seemed like the perfect chance to see if he'd want to move to Chicago.

"Autumn in the Windy City is a real nice place to be," Jim added as an incentive.

Ryan laughed. "Don't start telling me about the leaves changing color."

"They do."

Ryan chuckled. "I know they do."

"What do you say? I really would like you to come."

Ryan leaned back against the refrigerator, aware of the sudden concern in his friend's tone. "What's wrong there?"

"Nothing," Jim answered, then released a heavy sigh. "Okay, yeah, there is, or there might be. My sister is working on this case by herself, and like I said, it could get dangerous."

"And you're worried?"

"You got it," Jim admitted. "Hey, you've always wanted to meet her, haven't you?"

"Meg?"

"Yeah, Meg. I have only one sister, remember? The one whose photograph you stole from me."

"I didn't steal it."

"I haven't seen it since we left Washington."

"It was love at first sight," Ryan said lightly, realizing how foolish that sounded. But he had to admit that he was curious to meet the woman he'd heard so much about. "I'll come," Ryan said suddenly.

"You will?"

"Uh—huh. I'll be there as soon as I work out time off here."

"Now, remember," Jim added reluctantly, "my office is a little small, but if you decide to stay, we'd manage fine. It has great possibilities."

Ryan laughed at what sounded like a sales pitch. "Great possibilities, huh?"

"You bet."

"I can hardly wait to see it," Ryan teased.

Chapter One

Meg Gallagher shuffled the file folders on her brother's desk. She set them aside in a neat pile. The rest of the office was a shambles. That didn't surprise her. Jim would never win an award for neatness. She glanced at her wristwatch. Midnight seemed an outrageous hour to be cleaning anything. Deciding to return in the morning to organize the office, she reached down to the floor for her purse and nearly jumped off the chair as the phone rang. It rang three times before she reached for it and gave a hesitant hello.

"It's nearly midnight, Meg," James Gallagher scolded without preamble. "What are you doing at my office?"

Meg cradled the telephone receiver between her shoulder and jaw and reached for the can of soda on her brother's desk. Smiling at his exasperated tone, she leaned back on his brown leather swivel chair and prepared herself for his well-meaning lecture on safety and the single woman. "First, tell me what you're doing making a telephone call at midnight. You have to be breaking a hospital rule. I know that patients aren't supposed to—"

"Never mind that," he interjected, obviously determined to be the interrogator.

Just as determined, Meg asked him another question first. "How did you know I was here?"

"I'm a private investigator. Remember? I tracked you down. When I called the house and got no answer, I decided to try my office number."

"Jim, you didn't have to panic."

"Of course, I did." Jim released a mirthless chuckle. "What do you expect from a retired police captain's son? Not getting you at home, I went . . ."

"Into a tailspin."

"I didn't call Mom or Dad and tell them you weren't home yet," he said rather proudly. "But if I hadn't found you at the office, I might have."

Meg swiveled her chair away from the desk to stare out the small office window at the dark sky. "Thank goodness you didn't, or they'd have driven in from the suburbs. And what for?" she asked irritably. "I'm fine, Jim," she assured him. "And did it ever occur to you that I might be on a date?"

"I'd have been glad to learn that. But I knew you weren't. Since Kevin . . ." His words trailed off.

Meg guessed that he regretted bringing up Kevin's name. "I went out with Elliott."

"Elliott Zondor is no date, Meg. The great magician looks on you as a captive audience of one."

Meg sensed their conversation was heading toward the absence of men in her life. She took control of the conversation before he could say more. "You had a stack of mail." Absently Meg raked her fingers through her dark hair. "I was worried you had a bill that needed to be paid, and I didn't want to come back here in the morning and find the phone and electrical services shut off."

Her concerned words sidetracked him. "Well, I really appreciate your volunteering to help out, Meg, while I'm stuck in the hospital, but the whole family will break my other leg if a hair on that pretty dark head of yours is harmed."

"What are you so concerned about?" Meg questioned between slurps on the straw. Her eyes scanned the postage-stamp-size office that contained a red vinyl chair, a row of filing cabinets, and the scratched secondhand desk. Though the room had a shabby edge, her brother's list of clients was growing and he was happy at his work. "Jim, there's nothing here to steal," she added while staring at the monstrous black Royal typewriter that probably performed at its best in 1945. "It's not as if your last case belonged in a Mickey Spillane book. I doubt someone is going to barge in here with a machine gun."

"The building is empty, the alley next to the building is dark, the..."

"I'm not in the alley."

"You might have to pass it to get to your car."

Meg gave her head an exasperated shake. "I don't, and Chicago streets are well lighted, but—" she rushed the words "—I'm leaving. As soon as I set down the receiver, I'll go home."

"Good. And... Oh, damn."

"What's the matter?"

"It's curtains here, kid. The warden just walked in. The nurse with the Mr. Magoo face," he said more softly. "Bye."

Meg chuckled. "Bye."

Setting down the receiver, she shook her head. For a twenty-eight-year-old swinging single, he'd begun acting like a matronly aunt about her ever since she'd moved out of her parents' North Chicago suburban home four months before and into the city house that their grandmother had owned. Though Meg shared the same address with her brother, they lived in different houses. When Meg had agreed to take over caring for her grandmother's house, Jim had moved his things to the guest house at the back of the property. He'd said he wanted to give her privacy. Meg knew differently. He wanted to stay close enough to watch over her but not close enough for her to interfere with his bachelor activities. At twenty-two, she felt he was overdoing the big-brother act, but she knew that love motivated him. Good-naturedly, she'd learned to accept his and the rest of the family's overprotectiveness. It wasn't surprising—she was the first girl to be born into the Gallagher family in three generations.

While the position spoiled her a little, it also carried a burden. Everyone looked out for her. Though she never doubted her ability to take care of herself, she hadn't resisted them during this past year—since Kevin's death.

She and Kevin hadn't made any definite plans, but they had begun discussing marriage the week before that fatal October night. A motorcycle policeman, Kevin had responded to a routine call. Policemen handled domestic quarrels daily. But instead of a couple who were irate with each other, Kevin had walked in on a drug transaction and was killed. For a brief time after his death, she had leaned on her family not for protection but for strength.

They had shielded her from the media; and though she'd attended the funeral, she'd left immediately after it to visit an aunt in California. She'd needed time to heal and to sort out her life.

When she'd returned home, she'd made a few decisions. Though she'd previously planned on police work, she dropped out of the police academy and began taking classes to be an investigator for one of the government offices. Her other decision required less effort but was the stronger resolution.

Meg vowed never to fall in love with a policeman again.

And she wouldn't, she reminded herself while sliding a phone bill into her purse. It was an odd resolution for a woman born into a family of policemen. Law enforcement and the Gallagher name went hand in hand. Three uncles and her father had been cops. One brother was a lawyer, the other a probation officer and Jim was a private investigator. For her to do anything but law-enforcement work had always seemed almost sacrilegious to Meg. That was why she'd wanted to be a police-woman. But Kevin's death had changed that goal, making her realize that some careers carried higher risks. Unable to turn her back on law enforcement, she'd chosen a safer job as an investigator. She wanted her life free of the worry and the heartache associated with a high-risk job.

Despite Jim's concern for her safety, she didn't take unnecessary chances. Though she'd revealed an adventurous streak as a child and had preferred climbing the block-wall fence with her brother and cousins to playing with dolls, as an adult, she'd curbed that hint of daring in her personality. She'd driven with her seat belt on from the day she'd learned to drive, she dead-bolted her doors, and she never went to singles' bars. She even carried a vial of Mace in her purse, she mused as she slid two manila file folders into the center drawer of the desk.

Since she didn't believe in vampires popping out of their coffins at midnight, she considered lack of sleep her biggest concern at the moment. The whimsical thought made her smile as she glanced at the clock on the desk. Her brother worried unnecessarily, she decided, looking into her shoulder bag for her car keys.

Her fingers closed over them, but she stilled suddenly, alert to the sounds of footsteps outside the door. The shadow of a man flashed in the frosted window of the office door seconds before Meg saw his silhouette.

All of her brother's anxious words rushed back to her. The building was empty. She'd entered it with her brother's key, relocking the building's entry door before getting into the elevator. She had, hadn't she? Yes, she had, Meg assured herself. The man had to be renting one of the offices to have a key to the main door. But what if he didn't? What if he'd broken in? The unanswered questions quickened her breaths. Deciding to take no chances, Meg kept her eyes on the door while she fumbled in her purse for the desk keys. As the doorknob turned, she quickly slipped a key into the lock of the top desk drawer and reached in, closing her hand over the grip of her brother's revolver.

The man standing on the other side of the door seemed to fill the doorway. At least, she imagined that he did. Frightened, she knew that she saw him bigger than he was. Still, he stood over six feet. From the muscular shape of his build, she knew he was probably in his twenties or thirties. Making quick observations was one of the first things she'd learned at the police academy. Though she knew what to do if confronted by an assailant who might have a gun, her mind was a jumble of different thoughts. She could see the newspapers in the morning. Retired police captain's daughter killed in a gunfight. Calm down. Calm down, Meg reminded herself. He might not have a gun. But he could have one, she thought again. As she tightened her fingers around the handle, the cold metal beneath her palm sent a shiver of dread through her. Meg watched the door swing open and yelled out, "Okay, freeze."

Though he stopped cold, Meg heard his startled, confused laugh.

"Freeze. Stand still. Don't move," Meg ordered, her words rapid-fire as she held the gun out in front of her with two hands. "Now, take two steps forward. Just two."

"Wait a minute."

"Do what I said," she commanded as steadily as possible.

For a long moment, Ryan stood still and peered into the room. Speculatively, he let his eyes scan the office. Small, efficient, no frills, it was a man's office not a woman's. A desk lamp offered him a clear view of the woman behind the desk. He needed no introduction. Though he was a stranger to her, he knew Jim Gallagher's sister on sight. He'd seen her in his mind for the past few years. He felt a masculine urge to rush forward and put his arms around her as if they shared the familiarity of friends. But they'd never shared anything. They'd never met before this moment. Still, he knew her favorite color was blue; he knew that as a child she'd had a cocker spaniel named Loverboy; he knew she liked raking leaves and spending hours in the mystery section of the library. More importantly, he knew she made a point of never dating a cop. "What are you doing here?"

he asked while taking the two steps forward she had commanded.

He had a deep, no-nonsense voice, a voice like her father's. "That's my question," she said as the light from the desk lamp fell across his face.

Disconcerted, she watched him glance at the gun in her hands. Her heart pounded harder, fear skittering over her that he might dive at the gun to disarm her.

He looked in control, confident, a man certain of his ability to handle the unexpected. In a quick, sweeping perusal, Meg had already noted that he was in his late twenties and dressed casually. Beneath the unzipped winter parka he wore a pale blue cable-knit sweater. His jeans were dark blue but comfortable looking, and his sneakers were an expensive brand name. She realized now that her earlier assessment of his height had been incorrect. Just six feet, he'd appeared taller because of a rangy build. Her eyes traveled over his dark reddish-brown hair. It was neatly cut; the side strands brushed the tips of his ears. His strong features and the cleft above his lips gave him a stubborn, insolently sure look. She watched a dimple that emphasized one corner of his lips. The amusement in his navy-blue eyes assured her that her once-over hadn't passed unnoticed by him. She struggled to regain the controlling position and poked the gun at the air. "Start talking. Who are you? And what are you doing here?"

"Why don't you put that down before you shoot it. Or do you plan to?" He took a step closer toward the desk, never taking his eyes off the gun. "I'm a friend of Jim's." As she cocked a skeptical brow at him, he watched her lower the barrel of the gun and aim it in the vicinity of his groin and right thigh. "Brady. Ryan Brady," he added.

Meg stilled over the familiar name. Her brother had often talked about Ryan. They'd met in the marines and had become good friends. Though a flicker of relief flashed through her, she kept a sturdy grip on the gun. "Let me see some identification." As he reached toward his back pocket for his wallet, Meg ordered, "Slow."

Admiration mingled in with Ryan's amusement. She knew exactly what she was doing, he thought while flipping open the slim wallet and holding it out toward her.

Meg leaned forward on the desk, glanced at the photo on his driver's license, checked his name, and quickly let her eyes slide over the rest of the information: six feet, 170 pounds, twenty-eight years old. Heaving a long sigh, she leaned back in the chair and clicked the gun's safety catch back in place. "Jim's mentioned you a lot of times. I'm his sister. He's in the hospital. Did you know that?"

Again, he looked around the room. His friend chose comfort, not class. It was an office Ryan knew he'd be comfortable in, too. He was used to no frills in his job. His gaze returned to her. Dark hair framed her face, emphasizing her features. For a second he stared at her lips. They were expressive. Bow-shaped, pouting lips that with the slightest movement altered her innocent expression to a provocative one. "I talked to Jim," Ryan finally answered.

Though Meg looked down to set the gun in the drawer, she noted his softer tone. The stern, don't-dare-me sound definitely was gone.

"He briefed me on his injury. Since I had a few weeks' vacation coming, I told him I'd handle one of his clients. The harassment case," he added as explanation.

"You're from..." Meg paused, searching her mind. "New Mexico?"

"Albuquerque. I got in an hour ago and decided to see where the office was. When I came by, I saw the light."

"And decided to investigate?"

His smile came quickly. Boyish and amused. "That's what I do."

Meg sent him an inquiring look. "You're a cop?"

"A police detective. A sergeant," Ryan added. He leaned forward, bracing his hands on the desk, and watched her closely. He knew the answer to his next question before he asked it. "Do you have a problem with that?"

Meg shook her head. "No," she answered, but in her mind, Ryan Brady slid to the top of her ineligible list.

"Why do I hear a silent 'but'?"

He was far more perceptive than Meg had expected him to be. "I don't get involved with cops."

He smiled. A disarming, dimpled smile. "Were you thinking of getting involved with me?"

"No," she said quietly, though he'd rattled her. She reminded herself that he had an unspoken edge. Because of his job, he was well trained at making people squirm. Well, he'd met his match, she decided with determination. "Jim never told me you were coming here to help out."

With an ease that surprised him, she'd redirected their conversation. She wasn't easily led, he concluded, his admiration growing. "I talked to him only a few hours ago and told him I would."

"Well, I talked to him minutes ago, and he didn't mention your coming. So leave your phone number and I'll call Jim in the morning. If what you're telling me is true, I'll get in touch with you then, and you can look over any of the files that you want."

"I don't have a phone number. I just arrived. I did tell you that, didn't I?"

Feeling his subtle intimidation, Meg nodded and looked down. She reached for one of her brother's business cards in the center drawer of the desk. "Here." She extended the card to him. "Call this number in the morning."

Though he made no move for only a second, it was the longest second she'd ever experienced. His eyes again met hers. "I don't need it."

Puzzlement knit her dark brows. "You have this number?"

"No. But I won't need it," he assured her, looking as if he knew something she didn't.

The look skittered a nervous tingle through her. Meg smothered it quickly. "Whatever," she said in answer to his strange response and cued him by directing her gaze toward the door.

Ryan grinned wide, liking her spirit. No dull woman, he decided, pleased by the discovery.

Meg breathed easier as he turned and strode toward the door. He had a slashing, direct stare that intimidated without his saying a word. But something else about him unnerved her.

Ryan curled his fingers around the doorknob and looked back at her. "It's late. Do you want me to wait? I could walk you to your car."

More than his question surprised her. His voice carried a gallant softness that gave her the impression he'd feel honored if she'd agree. Meg sloughed off the thought as a romanticizing one. "No, that's not necessary."

"No hassle. Honest," he assured her.

Meg couldn't help smiling.

He stalled another moment then flashed a grin. "You aren't going to, uh, take that gun as protection, are you?"

"I have Mace in my purse."

Laughter edged his voice. "A gift from your brother, no doubt. Come on. Let me walk you," he appealed.

Meg nodded agreeably. "All right."

She joined him at the door and locked the office. They shared a quiet elevator ride. The silence was the expected kind of two people who hardly knew each other.

The only car parked on the empty street besides her five-year-old blue Mustang was a twenty-year-old green sedan. "Is that your car?" Meg asked, wondering if the dented monster with the missing hubcap ran or if he'd pushed it to that spot.

"That's it."

Meg shot a quizzical look at him. Though she hardly knew him, she was certain she'd heard pride of ownership in his voice.

"She's something, isn't she? I picked her up at Rent-A-Wreck. But I'm going to see if I can buy her."

She held back a smile. "You'd seriously want to buy that?" she asked with a fling of her hand in the car's direction.

"Anyone would."

Not me, she thought instantly, but she wasn't surprised that this man was her brother's friend. If Jim liked something, he announced it to the world, not caring one bit if the rest of the world thought him a little crazy.

"Lock the door, Meg," Ryan requested as she slid behind the steering wheel.

"I . . . always do."

He slammed the door before she'd finished speaking. Meg frowned as she stared into her rearview mirror and watched him stroll toward his car. She hadn't told him her name. How much had Jim told him about her? Though her meeting with Ryan had been brief, he'd acted as if they'd known each other a long time. Strangers. They were strangers. Strangers who knew about each other, she admitted to herself while starting the car.

Her brother had talked often about his friends, especially Ryan Brady. After the marines, they both had tried out for special detail in Washington, D.C. They'd decided that guarding dignitaries was monotonous and slow work. Meg remembered now that Ryan had been the one to quit first, returning to his hometown in New Mexico to join the police force. When Jim had finally left the Washington job, he'd returned to Chicago, deciding to venture out on his own by starting a private-investigation business. Though miles had separated Jim and Ryan, their friendship had continued. They shared long-distance phone calls every month. And Meg knew that her brother had twice visited Ryan in Albuquerque. She sensed the loyalty between the men. She'd felt the strong physical draw Ryan Brady had on people. Even on her.

Meg gave her head a slow, disbelieving shake. Mary Margaret Gallagher, you're cracking up. He has a nice smile. That's all. A smile that softened his features. And he's sexy looking. Sexy men elicit response in women, she reasoned as she turned down the street toward the house her grandparents had lived in for nearly fifty years. On Chicago's North Side near Lake Michigan, the Irish neighborhood was old, but owner pride had kept the homes from joining the decaying houses to the south. While her parents had moved to the suburban North Shore, her grandparents had remained in the older neighborhood until their deaths. At that time, her eldest brother, Patrick, had moved in while he finished law school. After he'd married and left the house, her other brothers, Brian and Jim, had set up their bachelor quarters at the house. Brian had soon decided to get married, and he'd rented an apartment closer to work. Jim moved to the guest house at the back of the property, claiming he didn't want to live in the bigger house. Meg guessed that what he really didn't want was all the housekeeping.

But his decision had helped her. Declaring a need for independence, she moved into the house. It was an outrageously large old building, but no one in the family had wanted to sell it. It had sentimental value. It was the Gallaghers' home. A home always open to family and friends, Meg thought, pulling her car into the driveway beside the turn-of-the-century house.

Headlights from another car flashed in her rearview mirror, making her squint. Stunned by the unexpected light, Meg peered hard into the mirror, realizing as the lights dimmed that a car had parked behind her.

She didn't have to see it to know it was Ryan's. She'd heard the car rattle to a stop. Annoyance flared within her. What did he think he was doing? She didn't need a personal escort right up to her door. Meg switched off the ignition and pushed open the car door. Fuming, she stormed back toward his car to inform him that she had enough big brothers.

Standing beside his car, he had one hand in his jacket pocket. In his other hand he carried one large canvas bag. Beneath the moonlight, tinges of red glistened in his dark hair and his eyes appeared darker, almost fathomless. Meg mentally counted to ten as she drew closer. "Mr. Brady..."

"I see you made it home without whipping out your Mace."

"Yes," Meg responded slowly. "Why are you here?" She constantly seemed to be asking him that question.

"I'm staying here."

Her mouth dropped open. Staying? He'd said he was *staying*. "What do you mean, you're staying?" Meg asked, too flabbergasted even to pretend politeness.

"I need a roof over my head."

"I'm sure you do. But whatever made you think it was going to be *my* roof?" Meg glanced around her. The street was empty. The air was still with the quiet of midnight. She wished now that she'd gone straight to the house. She would have felt more in control if she were standing on one side of the front door and he were on the other.

"Your brother told me I could stay here."

"No." Meg shook her head wildly. "No. Maybe he asked you to come here. Maybe he asked you to take over the case. But *never* would Jim tell you that you could stay with me."

He sent her a tired look. "Now, I don't know if you're tired or not. But I am. And I'm too worn out to stand in the middle of the street and argue with you."

"I'm not letting you stay with me."

"All I want to do is go to bed."

Meg knew she'd blushed, but his words had come so unexpectedly. "I don't know you," she said in a firm tone that had cooled a few men's ardor over the years.

He reached into his jeans pocket. "Look," he said, holding up a key. "For the guest house, right?"

The silver key glittered under the streetlight. "Jim gave you the key to the guest house?"

"Yes."

"When?"

"When?" he parroted in exasperation. "What are you doing? Practicing to be a government interrogator? Do you always ask so many questions?"

Meg nearly smiled. His amusement was obvious, and he did look tired. But she couldn't relent without answers to all her questions. "If he's in the hospital and you haven't seen him, when did he give you the key?"

Releasing a long sigh, Ryan dropped the canvas bag to the sidewalk. "Last summer, he took a trip to Albuquerque. He stayed at my apartment there. He had a key made for me then. He said if I ever got to Chicago, I might need to use it because sometimes he had to leave town on a case."

"Oh." Meg watched his eyes. Though his voice had remained calm and courteous, impatience had narrowed his dark blue eyes. "Okay," she conceded. "I guess it's okay for you to stay. But tomorrow I'm checking out your story with Jim."

Ryan suppressed a grin as he bent to pick up the bag. He doubted she allowed many people to back her down. Though he knew from Jim that Meg relented often to family requests, Jim had admitted just as freely that she acted out of love. People didn't push his little sister around. Ryan had guessed that in the office. Her eyes had darkened with a challenge, silently stating she refused to let him intimidate her. Even now, she stood ramrod straight, alert and on guard. "Relax. I have a kid sister about your age."

If his words were meant to give her peace of mind, he failed. Meg bristled inwardly. Though she didn't consider herself a raving beauty, she'd usually drawn more positive reactions from the men she'd met. Soothing a bruised ego, she suddenly felt tired. She looked toward the guest house and pointed her hand. "Follow the cement walk bordered by those lilac bushes. The guest house is at the back of the property after the willow tree.''

''All right.''

Despite his acknowledgment, he stood still. Meg made herself look back at him and tipped her head questioningly. ''Is there something else you wanted to say?''

''Go in the house. If your brother knew I stood here and didn't watch you get safely in the house, I'd never hear the end of it.''

Meg shot him a withering glare. She whirled away and headed toward the front stairs while she battled an urge to whip out the vial of Mace and demonstrate her ability to take care of herself.

Ryan grimaced over the slam of the door. Anger wasn't the mood he'd hoped to awaken in her, but for now he'd accept that—any emotion but indifference. At least for a while. Heading toward the back of the house, his mind held on to the image of Meg's eyes. Deep violet-blue eyes.

He remembered they'd looked more blue than violet in the photograph. A photograph he'd seen of her years ago. A photograph that had imbedded her image in his mind.

Chapter Two

Meg strode into the kitchen and turned down the volume to shut out the sound of the morning disc jockey. As she picked up the receiver, she stood in indecision about calling her brother. Though all of the Gallaghers were brought up to rise early, eat a good breakfast and start the day with a smile, it really was too early to call him.

She dialed her mother's number instead, but she needed answers from Jim about Ryan Brady. And she wanted them soon. If her brother wasn't aware of Ryan's visit, she wanted to know that before Ryan comfortably settled into the guest house.

Waiting for her mother's telephone to ring, she stared out the kitchen window. The day was bright, sunny yet cold. Cold enough for a sweater, she thought, mulling over what to wear.

The voice greeting her was cheerful. Her mother woke with a smile and in high gear. As long as Meg could recall, she never remembered her mother waking any later than six in the morning. She'd always said that a person who slept late missed the best part of the day.

"Oh, Meg, I'm so glad you called," Grace Gallagher said, snapping Meg back from her reverie.

"Why?"

"Are you going to the Irishfest this year?"

"Yes."

"Alone?" Despite her mother's casual tone, a trace of maternal concern came through.

"I'd planned on meeting you and Dad there." Meg waited a second then added, "Elliott asked me to go to the dance with him, but I wasn't really in the mood for that."

"Are you...?" Her mother hesitated. "Are you all right?"

Meg spoke lightly to make sure she wasn't asked any more questions like that one. "Mom, I'm okay. But the dance last year was the last time I saw Kevin. I don't want to revive those memories."

"I understand."

Meg believed she really did.

"Then would you want to come to the house after the entertainment is over? Your brothers are coming. Jim can't, of course, but Patrick should be back in town by then."

"He's out of town?" Meg frowned. "I thought he had a court case coming up."

"He does. But before he goes to court to defend that girl, he's trying to find the witness who'll verify that the poor woman was in New York at the time of the crime."

"Oh."

"And your father is cooking," Grace added. "He'll be disappointed if you don't come."

"Dad is cooking?"

"Yes. He's started taking gourmet cooking lessons. A hobby since his retirement." Her voice lowered to a soft conspiratorial tone that resembled a friend's more than a parent's. "I'm glad to let him. After thirty-four years of cooking, it's nice to let someone else do it."

Meg laughed softly. "Can I bring anything?"

"No, nothing, dear. Will you come, then?"

"Yes, I'll be there," Meg answered.

"So it's your dime."

Meg's smile widened. "What?"

"You called me, dear."

"Right." Meg gave her head a shake. "I wondered if you were going to the hospital to see Jim."

"I'm going tomorrow. Your father and Brian will be there today."

"Oh, well." Meg paused, trying to decide mentally what to do before she mentioned it. "I have that book on glass staining that you asked me to get for you."

"Wonderful. I'm looking forward to getting started."

"But I have classes today."

"Don't be concerned. I'll get the book from you some other time."

Meg smiled, grateful for her mother's considerateness. "What if I leave the book at the hospital and you can get it from Jim?"

"That's fine," Grace replied easily.

"Okay. I'll call you soon."

"Yes, dear. And don't forget to take time to relax."

"Yes, mother," Meg said, smiling.

"I know, I know, you're a big girl now."

"Thanks for worrying. Bye now." Meg set down the receiver and released a soft laugh. Whether her children were two or thirty-two, her mother would never stop worrying.

But Meg felt fortunate. During her growing-up years, she had never known estrangement from her family, even during the difficult teen years. Her parents had tried hard to understand rock music and fads. They'd known when to give their children freedom to spread their wings and when to insist on restraints. Because of her parents' good sense, the family had always remained close, yet each member was his or her own person.

Her brothers were quite diverse personalities. Serious and proper in his manner, Patrick had chosen wisely to become a lawyer. Brian, the most thoughtful and sensitive of the three, had become a probation officer. And Jim. Meg smiled as she grabbed a rag and began dusting a table. Jim was the closest to her in age and humor. Flaky described him best. He'd gone merrily through life without any real purpose yet had managed to succeed.

Meg glanced at the grandfather clock in the hallway as she swept the dust rag across her grandmother's mahogany piano. Questioning Jim about his best friend might not please him, but she'd put off that phone call long enough, she decided, and went to the kitchen to dial the hospital number.

The phone rang once before Jim yawned a hello.

"Did I wake you?" Meg asked.

"Nope. I just finished breakfast," he answered on another yawn. "I think they doped me up with something for pain. I'm ready to go back to sleep."

"They probably did that so you'd sleep all day and not give them trouble."

"Funny. I see you got home safely last night."

"Yes." Meg cradled the receiver between her jaw and shoulder while she poured a glass of pineapple juice. "But I had a surprise visitor at the office before I left."

"What?" Jim suddenly sounded incredibly awake. "You had trouble?"

"No, not trouble. But I had a visitor. Did you know Ryan Brady was going to come to town?"

"Ryan's here already?"

"Yes. He said that you told him to take over the Elizabeth Howard harassment case."

"Yeah, that's right. I figured the other cases would hold for a couple of weeks. Insurance claims," he added as explanation. "You said that you'd handle the office work."

Meg gnawed at her thumbnail. "I really wanted to work on the Howard case."

"Come on, Sis, it could get dangerous. I can't have you handling that alone. Anyway, she might need twenty-four hour protection. There's no way to know how serious that case could get. Ryan can handle it. He's experienced."

For the moment Meg kept her disappointment to herself. "What about his job in Albuquerque?"

"He tacked a leave of absence onto his vacation," he answered on a soft moan. "Hold it a minute. I have to shift."

As he moaned again, Meg grimaced for him. "Are you all right?"

"Fine. I'm fine. It just takes some doing to move my backside around while my leg is hanging in the air."

Meg waited another second and drank her juice. When he released a long breath of air, she continued. "So he came to help out or he came for a vacation?"

"Both. He wanted to see Chicago, see if he liked it. And he offered to help me out at the same time. To tell you the truth..." He paused for a long moment. "I'm glad he's there with you. I know he'll watch out for you."

"Is that what you told him to do?" she asked, remembering Ryan's comment about her being like a kid sister to him.

"I didn't say anything like that. I just know him. He'd watch out for a woman. He's got old-fashioned views about men being around to protect women. Gallant." He chuckled. "He's gallant."

Meg rolled her eyes at her brother's delight with his own joke. "I have a family full of men like that. I don't need another big brother."

"I didn't say he wouldn't...well...wouldn't..."

His stumbling manner made her smile. "Take me to the guest house to show me his etchings?" Meg teased, "Isn't that the line you give your dates?"

"I did want to show them my drawings."

"Of course. That's the reason. Tell me," she baited, "did you ever draw *anything* on that sketch pad after you'd unexpectedly brought it home and announced you'd decided to take up drawing for a hobby?"

"Yes. I most certainly did."

"And what is that? What...what did you draw?"

"A bowl of fruit."

Meg burst into laughter. "Is this the same story Mom gets?"

"Yes." Humor danced in his voice. "Do you think she believes me?"

"No. She's too wise." Meg ran water into the glass and set it on the drain board. "Me, too. And I'm wise enough to help with the Howard case. If your recuperation takes longer than you expect, Ryan might have to leave before the case is settled. I need to be involved in it," she insisted while bending over and tossing the dust rag over a bucket in the sink cabinet. Her hand stilled on the cabinet door as Jim remained silent. "He's only staying for a while, isn't he?"

"I don't know how long he's staying. Why don't you talk to him about the case? See what he thinks."

"Uh-huh," Meg answered. Since she wasn't sure she even liked Ryan Brady, Meg held back a committing remark about working with him. But regardless of what Ryan thought, she planned on staying involved in the case. Having already made her decision, Meg considered the discussion closed. "Whatever," she responded lightly. "I'll try to get to the hospital to visit you today."

"I thought you had school this evening?"

"A late class."

"Well, if you get busy then just give me a ring."

"I will. And, Jim—" she softened her voice to a conspiratorial whisper "—don't pinch the nurses."

He moaned. "Who?" he asked, sounding starved for the sight of a female. "All I ever see is Mr. Magoo's sister," he said and gave her a groaning goodbye.

As Jim replaced the receiver, the hospital door swung open. His brother Brian preceded their father into the room.

"You look lousy," Brian observed as a greeting.

A heavyset, barrel-chested man, Michael Gallagher gave Brian a hard nudge in the arm. "That's no way to talk to someone who's ill, especially your brother."

"Yeah," Jim agreed from the bed.

Brian's thin face widened with a smile. "He's not ill. He has a broken leg."

With his deadpan expression, their father quipped, "They shoot horses with broken legs, don't they?"

"I'm not *that* sick," Jim reminded him.

"Your mother thinks so," his father said, settling his bulky frame in a chair beside the bed and setting the large paper bag he'd brought with him onto the floor.

"What's in there?" Jim asked curiously.

Brian pulled a chair closer to the bed. "Your CARE package from Mom."

Their father nodded his dark head. Silver strands weaved through the dark ones at his temples. "Your mother said that when we were here yesterday she thought that you looked thinner."

Jim laughed at the look on his father's face as he frowned down into the bag. "You wouldn't have a beer and a pizza in there, would you?"

"Hardly," his father answered. "Let's see," he said reflectively. "Your mother sent banana bread so you'd get your potassium, dried fruit for vitamin C and..."

"Chicken soup," Jim finished knowingly.

Brian chuckled. "You guessed it."

Jim gave his head a slow shake. "One of my favorites," he grumbled, rolling his eyes.

Brian tapped the mattress to get his attention. "Patrick isn't in town, but he sent you a book."

"Some kind of self-motivation book?" Jim asked.

"If you keep guessing so well, you're going to get a prize."

"Patrick means well," their father stated firmly.

Jim shifted his shoulders on the mattress, trying to get more comfortable. "I know he does, Dad. And you?" he asked his brother Brian. "What did you bring me?"

He gave Jim a cocky grin. "A jar of peanuts."

"Bless you."

"So even though you look lousy, how do you feel?"

"Not too bad," Jim answered. "Just tired all the time. Too much medicine." He gave them a quick grin. "But

I'm glad you both came. I've been so bored I've begun to count the ceiling's acoustical tiles.''

"Has your sister been here this morning?''

Jim shook his head. "I just finished talking to her. She might come later today. She's going to take care of the office for me.''

"Why don't you look pleased?''

"I am. I mean I'm grateful that she volunteered, but I have one case that I'd prefer she didn't work on, at least not alone.'' As his father's brow furrowed, Jim assured him, "It's okay though. Ryan Brady came to help out. You remember meeting him, don't you? When you and Mom visited me while I was working in Washington?''

His father nodded. "I remember him. Nice fellow.''

"Isn't that the guy who you told me always asked about Meg?'' Brian questioned.

"Yeah. I started sharing letters with him when we were in the marines. I think he began getting interested in her then.''

"And now they've met,'' his father said in a speculative tone.

Jim made a face. "At the moment, she's not too thrilled with him being here.''

"She's adaptable,'' Brian said unnecessarily.

"Yeah, I know she is,'' Jim agreed. "But I wasn't only talking about the office work. Ryan might be thinking about them getting to know each other more personally. And you know how Meg feels about dating cops now.''

A frown flashed across his father's face. "All because of Kevin. She needs to know the truth about him. Why he died.''

"I agree,'' Jim said. "But how do we tell her about him now after all this time?''

Their father shrugged a shoulder, appearing lost for an answer to a problem for the first time in his life. He was a decisive man, a man of action, and Jim could see that not knowing how to handle the problem was gnawing at him. It was weighing heavily on everyone.

Michael Gallagher's blue eyes shifted from one son to the other. "I don't know how, but now I know that not telling her isn't fair to her. At the time of Kevin's death, we all believed that if we told her the truth it would be too painful for her to deal with, and she might stop trusting her own judgment. But now, now I know that she's being hurt more by our keeping the truth from her. She has to be told."

After showering and dressing, Meg headed toward the guest house. She made an honest effort to fulfill her promise of seeing Ryan after talking with her brother. Seven times she rapped on the guest-house door before she gave up and headed for the bus stop. But inwardly she was glad she hadn't reached him. She wanted time alone in Jim's office; she wanted Ryan to realize she was involved in the case, too.

By the time she reached the office building, it was past eleven. Located on a side street, less than a block from Michigan Avenue, the building was old, and the businesses inside were less prosperous than those in downtown Chicago's glass and stone skyscrapers. The red brick building's directory revealed a diversity of occupants: a locksmith, a telephone answering service, a jewelry wholesale company and a European auto leasing company. The office next door to her brother's private-investigation business belonged to Zondor the Great.

A magician, Elliott Zondor was a flamboyant man in his late twenties, who strutted down the building's hallway, swirling his cape around him. When he was seven, he'd seen the movie of Houdini's life. From that day on, he'd been hooked on magic. Though he worked part-time shelving books at the library, he saw himself as the next great magician of the world. Meg saw him as an actor— always on stage.

When she entered the office building, he turned away from the elevators to greet her. He raised his face and sniffed exaggeratedly at the air. "Been to the deli again?"

Meg stopped beside him and raised the white bag she held. "How can you always tell even before you see the bag?"

Beneath a skimpy-looking, sandy-blond mustache, his lips twitched with a smile. "I am a man of extraordinary powers."

Amused, Meg gave her head a shake. "One of your senses in particular is keener than the rest."

"Zimmerman's has the strongest-smelling kosher pickles in town," he added as the elevator doors opened. He swept his arm forward for her to precede him.

Meg waited until he joined her in the elevator. "And can you tell me what's in this bag?"

Immediately he pressed his fingertips to his forehead and closed his eyes as if in a hypnotic trance. "Ah, yes, it's very clear. Cream soda and a corned beef on rye."

"Amazing!" Meg said on a teasing note as the elevator doors closed.

"I hear the voice of a doubting Thomas."

"Probably because I know that you know I love corned beef on rye."

"You're going to ruin my image, love."

For the next few moments, he entertained her, waving a hand across his top hat. The rabbit never popped out of it, but he persevered until his fingers stretched sufficiently to lift the hat lining and find the paper flowers hidden there.

"I'll have to work a little harder on that for tonight's act," he said, frowning into the empty top hat.

"You're performing somewhere this evening?"

"A children's birthday party. And," he added excitedly, "I was asked to entertain at the Halloween Irishfest celebration."

"That's wonderful news," Meg agreed, smiling, but a tinge of melancholy swept through her as her mind flashed a memory back of her dancing with Kevin. It was the last date that they'd had together. The ache she'd felt no longer burned inside her constantly, but since that particular October night, she'd needed to be with people who were close to her.

She liked Elliott, had gone on late-night coffee dates with him, and considered a magician a remarkably safe occupation, but she'd never even felt her heart flutter when she was with him. Still, he did make her laugh.

Smiling over his last foiled trick, Meg unbuttoned her coat as the elevator doors opened.

Elliott followed her into the long hallway of connecting offices. "How long does your brother expect to be in the hospital?"

"A few weeks."

"Are you handling all of his cases?"

Meg shook her head. "Not really, but there is one that is extremely important. One of my brother's friends is here to help with it."

"That's good, isn't it?"

Meg saw his brows knit, making her realize that she was frowning. "I don't know if that is or not," she admitted. "It's not easy working with a stranger."

He gave her an understanding nod. "Love, I know that better than anyone. Lana's been sick off and on for weeks with some recurring flu. Finding a good assistant is not easy." He answered Meg's smile with a wink. "I know you don't want me to ask you again."

"No, it's not that," Meg said quickly. "I wish I could have helped you out more often, but I just haven't had the time."

"You've been more than helpful in the past. But I don't have to ask you to help tonight," he assured her, turning toward his office door. "I talked to Lana last night. She was well." He slipped the key into the lock. "All I have to do now is rehearse for tonight."

Meg nodded. "See you. And good luck," she called back, continuing down the hallway toward Jim's office while rummaging through her purse for the office key. As she drew closer to the door, her steps slowed. The soulful, wailing sounds of a jazz trumpet drifted into the hallway from Jim's office. Too many thoughts raced through her mind for her to concentrate on one as she rushed forward and flung open the door.

Sitting behind her brother's desk, Ryan looked up. He watched annoyance darken the color of her eyes and prepared for a trace of the well-known Gallagher Irish temper. As Meg closed the door behind her, he reached forward and turned down the volume dial on the radio. His eyes sliced to the bag in her hand. He sniffed hard once, easily identifying the contents of the bag as kosher pickles and corned beef.

Watching him hold down a smile, Meg grimaced, aware she was turning Jim's office into the delicatessen annex. "I thought you were going to wait until I called you."

"Never said that."

His gaze fixed for only a second on her lips. But it was a long second. Too long for Meg. The look fluttered something inside her.

"If something is worth waiting for, then I'm very patient." He gave the chair near him a push toward her. "Have a seat—*partner*."

Chapter Three

Meg eyed him warily. "Partner?"

"Jim said that you want to stay involved in this investigation." Leaning back in the chair, he folded his hands behind his head. Patience came easily to him. He'd been taught it early. Two younger sisters had constantly hogged the bathroom. The marines had programmed him to hurry up, get in line and wait. And the police academy had taught him that only a stupid cop didn't learn to bide his time. Waiting seemed almost like a game to him now. When he and Jim went fishing, Ryan always caught more because he saw the waiting as a challenge. Sometimes the one who made the first move would lose. He liked being a winner. Whether he was playing a game of chess or staking out a criminal. And he planned on winning now, too.

While he sprawled in a relaxed fashion behind her brother's desk, Meg stood by the door. She felt tense, as if she were the intruder in Jim's office. He studied her.

Though the look wasn't offensive, Meg felt the caress of his gaze on her flesh. Her green-and-black-striped boat-neck sweater with its wide, dropped-shoulder sleeves hung loose and enveloped her curves. Yet warmth from his look spread through her. The feeling came without warning but wasn't one Meg couldn't identify. This man had a startling effect on her. Even a look from him seemed to seduce. She battled the sensuality of that look as it drifted through the air between them. She'd met plenty of Jim's friends. Some were handsome, some were filled with charm, and she'd never allowed a look or a simple comment from any of them to unravel her. "And you have no objections?"

"Why would I?" His question came out on a smile. "Although I doubt you'll do well on surveillance work."

Lord, but she hated it when people underestimated her ability. "I've had some surveillance experience."

"In disguise?"

"What?"

"Did you wear a disguise?"

Meg frowned in puzzlement. "No. Why?"

"Because a private investigator needs to have an or-dinary appearance that allows him—or her—to get lost in a crowd." A grin tugged at the corners of his lips again. "You're far too pretty not to turn heads, Meg. Only a blind person wouldn't notice you the moment you walked into a room."

Meg blushed at his words. She hadn't expected them. The compliment stirred a self-conscious laugh. "Do you think *you're* ordinary looking?"

Dimples cut deeper into his cheeks. "Do you think I'd turn female heads?"

He knew darn well he did. She hadn't meant to tell him that she found him attractive. Although she needed distance from him, Meg forced herself to cross the room slowly. She plopped the deli bag on top of the filing cabinet. Her back to him, she yanked open the file cabinet and riffled through the manila file folders. "You'll want to see the Elizabeth Howard file." Meg looked back to see him pushing the chair away from the desk.

Morning sunlight glared into the room and highlighted the auburn strands in his brown hair. Strands the color of deep, dark copper. Glossy, they looked like silk. In her whole life, she'd never wondered about the texture of a man's hair, never felt an urge, an undeniable uncontrollable urge to touch someone. Her imagination was playing some crazy game with her, she decided, pulling the Howard file folder from its slot in the drawer. "Here it is." Meg slammed the file drawer and then rounded the opposite side of the desk.

As she opened the file folder, Ryan leaned forward and squinted at the paper. "Your brother told me that she's being harassed."

"Yes, she . . ." Meg made the mistake of looking up. Soft. His voice carried a soft, lulling quality. He had charm, a subtle, irresistible charm that stripped away a woman's resistance, made her feel unthreatened, yet left her vulnerable. She straightened so that his breath no longer fluttered heat across her face.

Though she'd placed space between them, he remained close. He sat on the edge of the desk, his hand resting near the top of the manila file folder. Meg fixed her eyes on her brother's chicken-scratch notes. Touching the top of the paper, she directed the moment back to his previous question. "What do you want to know about Elizabeth?"

His hand covered hers, stilling her. "No, tell me about Jim's accident. How did it happen? Was he involved in this case?"

His questions fluttered around in her mind. Despite her good intentions, she had trouble concentrating and answering coherently. All her thoughts centered on the masculine hand that had closed over the top of hers. It was a large, strong hand. Though not soft, his palm was smooth. Long fingers meant for playing a musical instrument gripped firmly but unbruisingly. She amazed herself as she kept her voice steady. "Jim was working on a different case. A woman had lost her poodle."

His head reared back in surprise. "Your brother was looking for a missing dog?"

Meg returned his amused grin while nonchalantly slipping her hand free of his. "Literally. He found the dog, but Jim slipped on a patch of ice during the chase, fell and broke his leg."

Frowning, Ryan glanced out the small office window at the brick wall of an adjacent building and the gray sky surrounding it. Meteorologists had forecast rain for the fall day, not snow or hail. "There's no ice outside," he finally said, still looking puzzled. "Chicago hasn't had any yet, has it?"

Meg giggled as she realized he'd misunderstood. She shook her head. "No. He wasn't outside. He was chasing the dog in a meat-freezer storage building."

Ryan sat straighter. "A meat freezer?"

"Uh-huh. See, the poodle was like a child to its owner. The woman pampered the dog, including buying it a fifteen-thousand-dollar diamond dog collar."

Ryan whistled low. "And no reputable crook could resist such an easy take."

"You guessed it. One of the landscaping men at the woman's home joined forces with his friend...."

"A butcher?"

Meg flashed a smile, admiring his quickness. "Yes," she confirmed. "They stole the dog. When Jim tracked it down, the crooks were trying to fence the collar. Since they didn't have any money yet, they'd kept the dog and were planning to ransom it. The butcher still had the dog locked in a back room of his shop. When Jim opened the door, the dog took off into the meat freezer compartment. Jim chased after the poodle. There was one patch of ice in the room, and Jim found it."

Ryan shook his head. "What dumb luck."

"Yes. He was even angrier because he'd just started on the Elizabeth Howard case that day. Here," Meg said, handing him the paper containing Jim's notes.

His dark brows drew together as he narrowed his eyes and tried to read Jim's handwriting. He spent another moment staring at the paper then gave up and pointed at a notation. "What the hell does this say?"

Meg laughed. "I've always told him that the way he writes he should have been a doctor."

He handed the paper back to her. "Decode this, will you?"

She peered at the note. Her brother's scrambled words required full concentration. But Meg wondered if she could do that with Ryan continuing to stare at her. What did he see? He'd said that she was pretty. He'd also subtly told her that he looked on her as a kid sister. Meg wasn't stupid. Men *did not* look at their kid sisters like *that*.

"Having trouble?"

Plenty, Meg thought but shook her head in response to his question. "Elizabeth Howard came into Jim's office a week ago. She's twenty-five, lives in a fashionable high rise off Marine Drive. She's a model.''

"Pretty?"

Meg looked up. "I don't know. I've never met her. But if she's a model, she's probably beautiful."

Ryan watched her face as she looked back down at the paper. Soot-black lashes hooded her eyes. He doubted she realized how beautiful she was. He pointed at a notation on the paper. "Jim would make a comment. It's somewhere on the paper."

Meg zeroed in on a specific scrawled notation. "Yes. He wrote 'knockout.'"

Ryan grinned and urged, "Go on."

"According to Jim's notes, a week ago she came out of the hair salon and walked toward her car to find all her tires slashed. Elizabeth thought vandals had done the job. But someone did it again when her car was parked in the lot outside the modeling agency. And she's received five mysterious phone calls."

"Obscene?"

"No," Meg said, studying the words harder. "The calls were made between one and five in the morning, no one talked, and no heavy breathing," she added, looking up at him.

His head slightly bent, he stared at the typewriter in a far corner of the room. His eyes had narrowed and zeroed in on the machine as if it held the answers to questions.

Meg hesitated to break into his thoughts. "Shall I go on?"

His head snapped toward her. "Yes," he said with a seriousness she hadn't seen before.

"A few days ago, she returned home to her apartment to find out all her utility services had been stopped. No phone, no electric, no gas. When she called the utility companies, she was informed that they'd been told to stop her services.''

"Who told them? A man or a woman?"

"A man called."

"Has Howard noticed anyone following her?"

"According to this," Meg said, pointing at her brother's notes, "she hasn't."

"You said that she's a model?"

"Yes."

"Where does she model?"

Meg looked down again. "She's between actual jobs right now. She's been hired to model at the Classic Auto Show next month."

"When did she get the job?"

Meg frowned at him as she shrugged a shoulder. "What are you thinking?"

"That we need to know if her trouble began when she got this job or before it. Do you know the phone number for the hospital?"

Meg nodded.

"Call your brother."

While Meg pushed the buttons on the telephone, she watched Ryan wander around the room. He stopped and stared for a moment at a poster Jim had tacked on the inside door of the closet. The cartoon drawing on bright orange poster paper showed a turtle lounging in his chair, his feet on his desk. The desk was as cluttered as the room. Above the drawing were the words: Geniuses are never neat.

Ryan shot an amused grin over his shoulder at Meg. "Your brother knows himself well."

She made a face. "Yesterday, I found a moldy, half-eaten liverwurst sandwich in his top desk drawer. He is the sloppiest—'' She cut her words short as her brother growled a hello at her. "Hello, yourself. Problems?"

"Hi," he groaned. "They're either jamming thermometers in my mouth or needles in my backside. What can I do for you?"

"Ryan wants to talk to you."

At her words, he strode across the room and moved behind the desk to stand beside her. Meg relinquished the receiver to him and shifted her stance to move around him. He stood firm, forcing her to remain still, trapped between him and the corner of the wall.

His closeness rocked her. Even if he viewed her as more girl than woman, she saw a man, a very sexy man who made her aware of her own femininity every time he was near. If he wasn't a policeman, would she have swayed beneath the charm of his slow-forming smile and the sparkle of humor in his dark eyes? Meg pushed the speculative thought aside and searched her mind for a logical reason not to like him. Her eyes flew to the radio. A saxophone and a trumpet dueled through a blues song. Jazz. He liked it. She hated it, she thought, feeling some satisfaction at finding a reason, even if it was a feeble one.

"Pudge?"

The childhood nickname snapped Meg's eyes toward Ryan. She watched his gaze run down her body and inwardly groaned over the childhood moniker her brother had often and affectionately used.

"Okay." Ryan nodded. "Yeah, that's all I wanted to know." As he set the receiver back in place, he started to smile. "Pudge? Why does he call you Pudge?"

"It's a holdover from when we were kids." Meg made a face. "I was a roly-poly when I was younger."

"The nickname doesn't fit now."

"I'll kill him," Meg murmured.

"Don't." He perched on a corner of the desk, keeping her cornered. "He's a sick man. Anyway, your secret is safe with me."

"Is it?"

"Of course. Partners are close."

Meg sent him an amused look. "Not always." Deliberately, she swung their conversation back to business. "What did you find out from Jim? Did the trouble begin after she received the auto-show assignment?"

Ryan stifled a grin over her response. "The day after the show's coordinator called the agency and okayed her as one of the models."

"So there is a connection?"

"Seems to be. Jim called Elizabeth Howard the day after his accident. Nothing had changed. Though she hadn't seen anyone following her, she'd had more of the same kind of phone calls. And someone threw garbage at her front door."

Meg grimaced. "What a sickie."

"Jim spoke with her this morning and told her I was taking over the case. So I guess it's time to meet the lady. I have to go to the police department first and register for investigating. Want to come along?"

Meg did but wouldn't, sensing she shouldn't get too close to him. "I registered two days ago," she volunteered. "Anyway, I have school tonight, and I still have some studying to do," she lied.

"Night classes?"

"Yes," she answered unsteadily as he pushed away from the desk.

"What are you studying?"

"I'm taking police-science classes. To be an investigator," she added weakly. He leaned closer, placing a hand on the wall near her shoulder. She felt uneasy. "I have to leave," she insisted, her eyes darting to the clock on the desk. Over his shoulder, she saw Elliott standing in the doorway. His frown made her aware of how cozy she and Ryan looked.

In full regalia, dressed in his purple cape, purple shirt and matching tight pants with sequin trim, Elliott sent her a quizzical frown. "Is everything all right?"

Ryan swung a look back at him as Meg offered a hesitant smile. "Yes." Discreetly, she pushed a hand at Ryan's shoulder so he'd move out of her way. For less than a second, he stood firm and stared down at her. Meg read a promise in his eyes as they sliced to her lips. A promise that he'd kiss her. If not now, then later.

As he shifted his stance, Meg slipped around him to approach Elliott. "This is Ryan Brady, a friend of my brother's. He's filling in for Jim until he's out of the hospital." Meg waited while Ryan had stepped around the swivel chair and moved closer before she completed the introduction. "Elliott Zondor. He's in the office next to ours," Meg added with a calmness built on pure determination. "He's actually Zondor the Great, a magician."

"Illusionist," he corrected after shaking Ryan's hand. "And I need an assistant tonight, Meg. Lana is sick," he added, making a face.

"She still has the flu?"

He rolled his eyes. "She's pregnant. Could you help me out? Just for tonight?"

"She can't," Ryan interjected before Meg had a chance to answer. "She has school tonight."

Meg bristled over his take-charge attitude, but she had no defense. To avoid being with him, she'd used that excuse.

"Oh, too bad," Elliott lamented. "Since you've done it before, I was hoping... Oh, well," he said, shrugging his shoulders. "I'll have to hunt around then. Must go." His voice sang as he waved his cape with one hand and whirled away. "Next time, love."

Ryan stared at the closed door and battled annoyance over Elliott's endearment. "Love?" he asked, facing her.

"It's just a word he uses."

"Like hocus-pocus and abracadabra? Magic words?" He watched her eyes darken with irritation. The last thing he'd meant to do was anger her. He raised a hand in a halting gesture. "Sorry. It's none of my business if you have a thing for him."

"I don't have a thing for him." Meg knew her quick denial had revealed more than she'd meant to, and she wanted to kick herself. "I assist," she added in a less excitable tone.

"Doing what? Do you let him saw you in half?"

Meg couldn't help smiling. "No."

"Put you in a box and poke canes through your body?"

"No."

"Levitate you?"

Meg made a face. "No, he doesn't know how to do anything like that. He's really terrible," she added. "He can't even successfully pull a rabbit from a hat. But he tries so hard. He wants to be this decade's Houdini."

He heard sympathy and affection in her voice. Willingly she'd stand on stage beside a friend even though she knew he'd be less than successful in his magic act. A woman possessing such sensitivity had strength. "So what do you do in the act?" he asked, leaning over the desk and opening the manila file folder.

Meg watched him write Elizabeth Howard's address on a sheet of paper. "After I step into a trick box, he struts around on stage, waves his magic wand, and says something like abracadabra while I step through the trick door inside the box and disappear. When he lifts the lid on the box, I'm gone."

"Your friend Elliott obviously has learned that the power of suggestion *is* magic."

Without another word to her, Ryan headed toward the door. He'd learned a lot about timing, about stringing people out. Though he'd have preferred a more honest approach with her, at the moment he couldn't reveal how interested he really was in her. He swung the door open and glanced at the frosted glass in the door, at the letters painted across it. He squinted, visualizing them to read: Gallagher and Brady Investigation Service.

Meg stared quizzically at his back. As Ryan closed the door behind him, she wondered if her imagination had drummed up those cozy seconds before Elliott had walked in. Nervously, she touched her hair and then reached forward and turned the radio dial to a different station.

Ryan stepped into the hallway and smiled as jazz gave way to soft rock. Meg Gallagher definitely liked things her way. But so did he.

Chapter Four

Ryan looked up and past the semibare, tangled limbs of an oak tree. At seven in the morning, gray clouds hung low in the sky, promising a dismal, overcast autumn day. A crisp wind cut into his face as he closed the guest-house door behind him and started down the path that led toward the large gabled house. The ground felt soggy beneath his feet, and in a youthful gesture, he pushed the toe of his sneaker beneath a pile of leaves that were fiery with color.

Even before he saw light in the kitchen window, his thoughts were focused on the woman inside that kitchen. That didn't surprise him. Thoughts about Meg had haunted him for a long time. The photograph he'd seen of her had captured the beauty of her well-defined but delicately sculptured features, had revealed a classic beauty with strong cheekbones, but the photograph hadn't captured her sparkling charm or her smile. In fascination, he'd watched her smile barely curve the edges of her lips while she'd veiled some private amusement. It was a smile, a look that he knew he'd never tire of seeing.

He stopped on the back porch and listened to the music. Rock music at seven in the morning. A softer, feminine sound accompanied the raspy voice of the rock singer. Ryan smiled wryly and rapped on the door, expecting Meg to greet him with a bright smile.

Meg turned away from the bacon sizzling in the frying pan and opened the door. Nerves tensed. The reaction was so immediate, so powerful that she had to force a greeting. "Good morning."

"Morning." He saw a hint of nervousness as she tucked her hand into the pocket of the pale blue robe. "Your brother didn't have any coffee. I wondered if I could borrow some?"

Meg shook her head and returned to the stove. "No."

"No?"

"Uh-uh. I don't have any."

"Made, you mean?" he asked, leaning a hand against the doorjamb.

"No, I mean I don't have any." Meg looked over her shoulder at him. "I don't like coffee." He sent her a look as if he thought she were crazy.

"No coffee? You don't have any in the house?"

Meg couldn't help smiling. He looked dumbfounded. "I don't like it. But would you like some juice?"

Ryan looked past her to the table. On top of a powder-blue place mat was a matching napkin, a blue-flowered plate, and a water goblet. "Uh, yeah. If it's no trouble."

"No." Meg stared down at the frying pan. "Would you like some breakfast, too?"

"Lord, no," Ryan groaned. He glanced sidelong at the eggs with their perfect yellow centers. "How can you even look at those things at seven in the morning?"

Meg held the spatula in midair. "You never eat eggs?"

"Sure. But not so early."

Meg laughed and faced him. "When?"

"At a sensible time of the morning. Like eleven."

"Eleven! That's when you eat breakfast?"

Ryan leaned his hips against the edge of the white Formica kitchen table. "Yeah. On days off, I try not to get up before that."

"When do you eat lunch?"

"When I get a chance."

"And dinner?"

"Same."

"No regular eating hours?" she asked, shaking her head disapprovingly as she anticipated his answer.

"No." His answer came out slowly. At her movement, the vee of the robe bellowed, and the swell of a breast caught his eye. Her flesh appeared softer and silkier than the pale blue cloth covering it. An unexpected emotion briefly clutched at his insides. Searching for any kind of distraction, he watched the swaying movement of her dark hair as she turned her head. Strands of brown silk brushed her shoulders, drawing his gaze back to the vee of her robe. Ryan gave his head a mental shake, but he was completely caught up in watching her.

She moved easily, like a woman who didn't believe in dainty feminine steps. When she turned and handed him the glass of juice, he noticed her hands: their softness, the slimness of her fingers, the shortness of her nails. His fingers closed over the tips of hers on the proffered glass. "Do you bite your nails?" Her answer was unimportant. What he'd needed was her touch.

Ryan sent her a pained look. "I was looking at that ... plant on the windowsill."

Meg shrugged her shoulders. "Its leaves keep falling off." Though she poked her fork at the eggs, her head snapped up as he bounded from the chair. In two strides he'd crossed the kitchen. Meg watched as he dabbed a finger at the soil in the pot.

"You waterlogged it."

Meg made a face over what sounded like an accusation. "I don't have a green thumb."

"Obviously." He frowned at the soil for a long moment before returning to the table. "Do you know how few people can't grow a philodendron?"

Meg narrowed her gaze. The dark blue eyes that met hers danced with humor. "Are you having fun?" she asked, glad she'd swallowed a curt retort.

Ryan chuckled. "You rile quickly, don't you?"

"I've been told that," Meg admitted. "And you tease often."

Her smile revealed more than her words. With three brothers, she was used to male teasing, knew how to accept it and, when necessary, knew how to banter back. "Bring the plant back to the guest house later. I'll show you what to do to revive it."

Meg looked up from her plate. No, she reminded herself. No involvement with him. No involvement of any kind. She was too susceptible, too vulnerable to this man, she realized. She'd sensed that from the moment they'd met. "You don't have to bother." Nervously, she bolted from the chair with her plate in her hands.

Meg turned on the water faucet and began washing the dishes. She knew he stood close behind her even before he reached around her to set the juice glass in the sudsy water. His words fanned strands of her hair near her temple.

"I'll talk to you later."

Meg simply nodded her head, keeping her eyes on the sponge in her hand as he strode toward the door. She tried to think about something, anything but him. She concentrated on the radio, on the raucous ending of a rock song, on the disc jockey's voice. Softer melodic sounds drifted from the radio. She concentrated on the familiar tune and hummed along with the mellow singer. She needed some sound other than the loud, excited beat of her heart. The message it was pounding out meant disaster if she kept listening to it.

She waited until she heard the latch of the door click, then turned around and leaned back against the kitchen sink. She laid a hand against her chest and felt the hard, quickened beat of her heart. An accelerated beat that warned her. She definitely had a problem.

Wanting to see her brother before her early-afternoon class, Meg hurriedly dressed. As she rushed toward the door to leave, her eyes rested on the collapsed philodendron. She grabbed it and took the nearly dead plant and a plastic garbage bag with her. Outside she lifted the garbage-can lid and dropped the bag into the can. Gently, ceremoniously, she laid the plant on top of the plastic bag. She didn't need to spend time with Ryan while he instructed her on how to nurture a dead plant back to life. He aroused a distinct reaction in her. She knew she was ready to fall in love again. But whoever that man was, he wouldn't be a policeman.

After finishing a few errands, Meg pulled into the hospital parking lot and hurried toward the entrance door. She juggled a best-selling espionage novel and a bag filled with hard candy while she reached for the handle of the glass door. Through the glass, she saw the huge clock above the hospital's directory. Her stops at the bookstore and the candy counter had taken longer than she'd expected. But she'd spend some time with her brother. Any time with him would help. She knew he was turning into the fifth floor's number-one grouch because he wanted to go home.

Passing the nurses' station on the orthopedic floor, Meg offered a quick smile. "Has my brother been giving anyone trouble today?"

The nurse behind the counter, a robust woman with a sour face, responded with a grimace that deepened the lines bracketing the corners of her mouth. "A little, until his breakfast came."

"He's used to eating breakfast earlier," Meg said with a laugh and kept walking. Blame our mother, she thought whimsically. No Gallagher ever started the day without a good breakfast. Since the hospital served Jim his at eight-thirty, they were already an hour off his normal schedule. He'd be grouchy she mused, realizing how set in his ways he was at twenty-eight.

With her shoulder, she pushed open the door to her brother's room. Instead of being on his back, his leg hiked in the air, he sat with pillows propped behind him. His leg, though still hanging in the air like a side of beef, seemed to be in a better position. By her brother's expression, he was indeed more comfortable.

A bright smile sprang to his face as she walked toward him. "Hey, Meg, you got here. What's in the bag?" he asked on the same breath, tipping his head slightly to the side to see what she held in her hand.

"You're worse now than you were when we were kids."

He looked aggrieved. "I was a good kid."

"You were not. You shook every package under the Christmas tree. Broke a few things, too."

"Forget about that."

He sent her a scowl that she found more amusing than threatening.

"What's in the bag?"

"Candy." Meg handed it to him. "I saw that you ate the whole bag that I left for you the other day. Your teeth are going to fall out."

He sent her a toothy smile. "No, they won't. I didn't eat it all by myself."

"Sure," Meg teased. "The nurse helped you."

"Ryan did."

Meg pulled the chair away from the wall and close to the bed. "When was he here?" she asked, trying to sound casual as she noticed a chess set on which the pawns had been moved.

"Still am."

The familiar voice coming from the doorway jolted her. Meg whipped around to look at him.

Ryan sauntered in, his eyes never leaving hers. "Are you discussing Jim's candy addiction?"

"Yours," Jim quipped back.

Meg strived for inconsequential conversation, anything to keep her mind free of the look he'd given her when he'd entered the room. "When you were a boy, did you shake presents that were under the tree?" she asked Ryan.

"Still do."

Meg sent him a smug look. "That's a contradiction. You told me you were a patient man."

"And I also told you that depends on what I'm waiting for." Dark blue eyes sparkled as he sent her a brief look. A look filled with teasing sensuality.

"I saw you one Christmas," Jim reminded him. "You ripped off the paper."

"I was helping my nephew that day."

"Ha!" Jim popped a peppermint candy into his mouth. "You wanted to see what he got almost as badly as he wanted to."

"I could tell that it was a baseball mitt," Ryan excused, walking toward the window.

Meg smiled over their bantering. "How many nephews?" she asked, curious, as she remembered that Jim had visited Ryan at Christmastime one year.

"Six. One niece."

"Whoever marries him better like being the mother of boys," Jim piped in.

Meg said nothing. But neither did Ryan. An uncomfortably long silence suddenly filled the hospital room—a silence filled with unspoken words between the two men, as Jim shot a prodding look at Ryan. He responded with a grin. One that Meg couldn't interpret. She only knew that for some reason her brother's comment hadn't been a casual one. Disturbed, she realized he'd said it for her benefit. Meg shifted uncomfortably on the chair. Whatever their exchanged look meant escaped her. At the moment, she didn't want to know. Sometimes ignorance was bliss, she decided, yanking the paperback from its bag and handing the book to Jim as she stood up.

"I have to leave. School," she added on a parting note before she stepped into the hallway. Why, she wondered, would her brother think she should be interested in that kind of information about Ryan? She gave her head a slow shake, refusing to ponder the question. But during her next visit to see Jim, she'd set him straight. She was not interested in Ryan Brady.

Ryan stood by the window and stared down at the sidewalk. Behind him, he heard Jim moan as he shifted.

"How are you doing?" Jim asked over the rustle of the bag as he reached into it for another piece of candy.

"Are you asking about the Elizabeth Howard case or about my romance with Meg Gallagher?" Ryan asked on a smile.

"My sister. I want to know how it's going with my sister."

"Not well."

"Told you that she'd freeze the minute she learned you were a policeman."

"It'll work out," Ryan said, watching Meg briskly stride away from the building. The wind whipped her hair forward around her face, nudged her away from him. Somehow, he'd convince her that she couldn't keep running away from her own feelings.

He knew she faced problems head on. He'd learned that from the letters she'd written to Jim. He'd liked that quality about her, admired her ability to take the good with the bad and make the best of a situation. He remembered one letter to Jim filled with bright excitement about her prom night. Her anticipation about her dress and the special evening had been obvious in her letters. The letter Jim had received after the prom had held pages filled with a funny story. Ryan had sensed her good nature then and her ability to laugh at herself as she'd told about the rainstorm, the puddles, and the boyfriend's car getting stuck in a muddy rut. By the time they reached the prom, she'd said, she looked as if she'd gone for a swim in the lake. But she'd had a wonderful time.

"Brady, you are one tenacious dude."

Ryan turned around and smiled. "Your fault."

"Mine?"

"You shouldn't have shown me her photograph." Each letter Jim had received had intensified Ryan's curiosity about Meg. He liked her, and he hadn't even met her. Then, during a long night while he and Jim had been guarding a Soviet dignitary in a home on one of Georgetown's narrow, tree-lined streets, Jim had shown him her photograph.

Ryan had seen more than her obvious beauty. The tilt of her chin declared her strong-willed spirit; the blue eyes that had the power to attract contained a sparkle of the good humor he'd heard in her letters. But he'd seen more. She smiled for the camera, but he'd felt her warmth, the caring within her that made her don a Santa Claus costume for her nieces and nephews and stuff pillows into her legs to create his roly-poly form. Ryan knew when he'd seen that photograph that he had to meet her.

Jim reached into the candy bag and tossed a butterscotch at him. "How was I to know you'd fall in love with her at first sight? You're a cop. You're supposed to be logical, analytical."

"I am."

"Not about Meg. How could you be so sure she'd be the right one for you?"

Ryan looked down and unwrapped the candy. "I wasn't sure."

"And now you are?"

Ryan raised his face and grinned.

"Have you said anything to her?"

"No! She'd think I was crazy. I'll just have to wait until she falls in love with me, too."

"What if she doesn't?" Seriousness clouded Jim's eyes. "What if she won't let herself?"

"Because I'm a cop?"

"Yeah."

"If she knew Kevin hadn't been as cautious and disciplined as she thought he'd been..." Ryan's words trailed off as he halted his own frustration about the problem.

Jim gave him an understanding nod. "If she knew that he'd ignored orders, she might feel differently about you."

"Hell, Jim, he wasn't a smart cop. He was responsible for placing his life in danger." Ryan shrugged. "But she doesn't know that."

Jim looked helpless. "No, she doesn't. And I don't know how to tell her now. No one does."

"Don't your parents think that she should be told?"

"Sure, they do."

"Soon?"

Ryan's snapped question made Jim grin. "Getting impatient?"

"A little," Ryan answered, but confidence edged his voice. "But I can wait. Whether you want me for a brother-in-law or not, I'm it."

Jim returned an easy grin. "I could do worse, I guess. And good fishing buddies aren't easy to come by."

While cooking a hamburger that evening, Meg stared out the kitchen window and thought about her problem. Ryan. Definitely he was her problem. As much as she wanted to get hands-on investigating experience by helping with the Howard case, she felt she had no choice except to stay away from him. Avoiding him seemed the most sensible action. But was that possible? she wondered as she stared out the kitchen window and watched him walking down the path toward the house. He battled a brisk wind that tossed his hair and molded his shirt against his chest. His strides were long, determined; and watching him, she sensed the unwavering firmness in his personality.

Meg took a step back away from the stove and the window as he stopped at the garbage can and lifted the lid to drop a bag into the can. For a long moment, he held the lid in midair. Unexplainable guilt rippled through Meg as she watched him walk back toward the guest house with her wilted philodendron cradled in his large hands. It's only a dumb plant, she reminded herself, but seeing him with it made her feel as if she'd done something catastrophic, like sold government plans to the enemy. Annoyed with her own reaction, she was even more certain that she shouldn't see him too often.

Chapter Five

Through the week, she succeeded in not talking to Ryan, but he didn't disappear from her life. Repeatedly, she saw him carrying green plants toward the guest house: ferns, giant split-leaf philodendrons, and rubber plants. While she wondered if he was turning the guest house into a jungle, she held firm to her resolution and stifled her curiosity to go see what he was doing with all those plants. Disconcerting to her, he seemed just as determined to insist on contact.

Daily, he tacked notes on her back door informing her about the investigation. Meg tried to pretend disinterest. But in his own way, he kept drawing her into the Elizabeth Howard case. He aroused her curiosity enough that on Thursday Meg left a note for him asking about Elizabeth Howard's boyfriends.

The next morning Ryan's note was short and direct: Check them out.

For the next three days between stopping at the office for the mail, attending classes and keeping pace with household chores, Meg tracked down the last three men in Elizabeth's life.

On the following Monday, Meg hurried from her afternoon classes to the grocery store. A can of coffee miraculously found its way into her shopping cart. She reasoned that just because she didn't like coffee didn't mean she shouldn't have any in the house. She unpacked the grocery bags, changed into her bowling shirt and black slacks, and rushed from the house in less than an hour's time.

Though she bowled ten pins over her average, Meg realized her mind had been elsewhere for the past couple of hours. Driving toward home, she wondered how Ryan spent his evenings—where he went, what he did, who he was with. She knew thinking too much about him was a mistake, but she kept right on doing that. His daily notes were pulling her even more toward him. Every morning she would rush down the stairs, pour herself a glass of juice and open the door to read his words. If he meant nothing to her, she realized, she'd be throwing the slips of paper away. Instead, she was neatly stacking them in a top drawer of her dresser as if they were love notes.

Stopping at a red light, Meg shook her head. She was her own worst enemy. As the light turned green, she sensed herself weakening—she wanted to see him. In her present mood, going home seemed a mistake. She whirled her car around and headed instead for a favorite restaurant—Clancy's.

Catering to Irish-Americans, Clancy's Pub provided a gathering place for families who clung to some Irish traditions. Though the clientele praised the cook's mulligan stew, people came with their families for the lively conversation, the gay music, and the Irish atmosphere.

The strong aroma of corned beef and cabbage greeted Meg as she opened the double doors with their stained-glass windows. She crossed the terrazzo floor, winding her way around dark oak tables and cane chairs with their padded seats.

Ryan stood by the end of the bar and watched her. For over a week, he'd made it easy for her to avoid seeing him, but he hadn't stopped thinking about her. Two years before she'd been involved with Kevin, and Ryan had kept his thoughts about her to a minimum. But when Kevin had died, Ryan had allowed his feelings to resurface. Still, Ryan had waited. Jim's accident had seemed like a twist of fate, a reason to come to Chicago, to meet her and to find out if those feelings were real. After all that time, Ryan knew now he hadn't been acting like a fool and wasting his time thinking about a woman he hadn't even met. Though younger than most of the women he'd dated, Meg enticed him. She had a zest for living that flared his interest. He sensed that he could stand with her in freezing cold weather with snow floating down over them and still feel her inner warmth. Though she stood a few feet away from him now, he felt a closeness with her. There was no logical reason for it. They hadn't known each other long, but he believed she was special.

Jammed with a Monday-night crowd, the interior was smoky and dark. Meg smelled a familiar woodsy aftershave and looked around her. Men were lined up two deep along the mahogany bar, but she didn't see the man whose face sprang to her mind. She gave her head an imperceptible shake, not believing the trick her imagination was playing on her.

As she continued to inch her way toward the smaller, dimly lighted back room designated for dining only, she smiled and talked to people she knew. She glanced toward the corpulent man behind the bar. Offering the same warmth and friendliness to patrons that his great-great-grandfather Padraic had shown, Sean Clancy sent her a bright smile. "No school tonight?"

Meg shook her head, not even trying to answer above the din in the room.

"You look like you're losing weight, Meg. Have some supper."

Meg smiled and nodded her head before inching her way to an unoccupied table for two in the far corner of the restaurant. She'd barely sat down when Sean Clancy's niece brought a green goblet of water and the glossy kelly-green menu to the table. "The stew," Meg requested without even glancing at the menu.

"Won't be a moment, Meg."

Slipping off her blue blazer, Meg scanned the room. Briefly, she watched two men challenging each other in a game of darts. She thought again about her school assignment, considered going to her car for a textbook and immediately discarded the thought. Overhead, a Tiffany lamp allowed only a minimum of light to reach the table. Relax, Meg told herself, watching Sean Clancy move through the crowd and mingle with customers.

"Is your brother healing?" the waitress asked.

Meg flashed her a smile. "Slowly. Too slowly to suit him."

"'Tis good his friend came then. Ryan," she added, setting the plate of stew before Meg.

Meg stared quizzically at her. "You know about him?"

"Oh, sure. A charmer, he is. And has your weakness for our specialty."

"He's been in here?"

"Often." She swung a smiling face toward the bar.

Meg inwardly groaned at the sight of Ryan leaning against the bar and grinning at her. When he pushed away from the bar and started winding his way around people to reach her, she felt anticipation sweep through her. Avoiding him suddenly seemed like an impossible task.

As he drew near, Meg inclined her head questioningly and worked for a nonchalant tone. "Hi. Do you want to join me?"

"That was why I came over."

"I checked out Elizabeth's boyfriends," she informed him to keep conversation on business.

"Good." Ryan sat across from her. "What did you find out?"

"She's had three boyfriends since moving here."

"From where?" he asked, setting his forearms on the table and hunching forward with interest.

"Los Angeles."

"Lovers?"

"One was a live-in boyfriend," Meg answered, pushing the fork tip into a piece of meat on her plate. But she doubted she'd be able to eat. He made her anxious, nervous. "He's a stockbroker. One of the others is a lawyer. She went with him about four months. The other one is an insurance broker. She dated him only a month."

As she stared down at the plate, Ryan inclined his head to see her face better in the dim light. She was deliberately avoiding his eyes. He was used to observing people. They avoided eye contact when they lied or when they were worried they'd reveal too much. "Did you check him out?" he asked, tempted to touch the fringe of bang covering one of her eyebrows.

"He's married. Was married then, too," Meg said behind a napkin as she dabbed at her lips.

"Did Elizabeth give him the boot?"

Setting the napkin on the table, she looked up. In the dimly lighted room, his eyes appeared darker as they slowly moved over her features and then focused on her lips. Though the buzz of voices and the din of raucous laughter filled the room, Meg felt enveloped in some private cocoon. She could hear only her own thundering heartbeat, see only the handsome man across from her, smell only his clean scent and the woodsy fragrance of his after-shave. Maddening, she thought. He had a maddening effect on her. "No. His rich wife threatened to divorce him if he didn't stop seeing Elizabeth."

His expression turned thoughtful. "The wife might..."

"She's pregnant," Meg added. "Due any day. I doubt she could bend down, much less slash someone's tires."

"What about the lawyer? Did he and Elizabeth split as friends?" he asked before taking a long swallow of beer.

"Definitely. He's still her lawyer."

Ryan released a heavy sigh. "We have a lot of dead ends. What about the lover?"

Meg broke free from his gaze as a different tempo of music filled the restaurant. "He's getting married next week." For a moment, she listened to the bright and lively sounds of an Irish jig. She kept her eyes on the couple dancing. People made space for them and clapped their hands to keep time with the couple's quick-moving steps.

"Do you know how to do that?" Ryan asked.

Meg wrinkled her nose. "Not well. Can you?"

"Poorly."

Meg flashed a smile back at him. "So what do you think?" she asked, deferring to his experience. "Could the live-in still be angry about something?"

His eyes flicked briefly to her lips. "Why do you keep avoiding the word 'lover'?"

Meg wanted to let his question pass, but the steady blue gaze fixed on her carried a challenge. "Elizabeth didn't call him that. She said that she lived with him."

"Live-in and lover are usually one in the same."

Meg shrugged one shoulder noncommittally.

"Have you ever?"

Her eyes snapped up from her plate. "What?"

"Lived with anyone?"

"No!" She whipped the answer back at him and inwardly felt the heat of a blush. Fighting it, she shot the question back at him. "Have you?"

"Yes."

The music of an accordionist overshadowed his monosyllabic response, stopping Meg from asking more. But her mind was busy. She wondered about the private side of him. On the surface, he was easygoing, quick to smile and easily amused. She knew that as a policeman that he had a serious side. She'd briefly seen his experience from that job as they talked about Elizabeth. But what about him—the man? She knew that he ate no breakfast and liked jazz. And he believed in coddling plants. That gentleness, that caring made him different. She sensed a man who understood tenderness, who believed in romance.

But the room was filled with other young men, she reminded herself. Some of them were just as handsome and just as charming, yet none of them made her react with a mere touch or the teasing hint of a smile. He did that to her in ways far more dangerous than she would have expected.

She stared at the couples step-dancing. Standing side by side, hands joined, one young couple seemed caught up in a challenge as their steps grew quicker. But as fast as their feet were moving, Meg noticed their eyes never shifted away from each other. The love between them sparked the room with a current of excitement. One by one, the other people stopped dancing, becoming as caught up in the enchantment of the couple's mood as in the magic of their feet.

When the music stopped, they breathlessly hugged each other, but Meg noted that their joy sprang from each other, not from the applause.

The room filled with other sounds again, men turning back to lean on the bar and lift their beer mugs, diners picking up forks and returning to their meals. Everyone was forgetting the magic of those moments, but Meg couldn't. She felt Ryan's eyes on her. Susceptible to the smile that quickly sprang to them and to his lips, she continued to scan the room. Peripherally, she saw Sean Clancy approaching their table.

"Will you favor us with a tune, Ryan?" Sean asked, handing him a flute.

Ryan stared at it for a long moment. During his youth, he'd practiced playing it, but he'd always felt youthful displeasure. His father had insisted that he learn to play it well. In his booming voice, he'd told Ryan that someday he'd be grateful. Someday when he'd want to tell a woman what he felt for her and words didn't come easily between them, he could let the music tell her. At ten, Ryan hadn't understood. Now, he did. He brought the flute toward his mouth and began playing, knowing now his father had told him the truth.

Meg couldn't veil her surprise. Though she'd thought he had musician's hands, she'd never have guessed that he'd play something as fragile-sounding as a flute.

The slim, delicate-looking instrument looked strange in his large hands. Over the top of the flute, Ryan's eyes smiled at Meg. Pleasure mingled with her surprise while he played. The soft, shrilling notes floated in the air, quieting the crowd, turning their attention on him, but he never took his eyes from her. Every note of the slow Irish love song seemed meant for her. He is a charmer, Meg thought, unable to suppress a feeling that he was playing the song for only her.

She scarcely breathed as he drew the notes out to lull the listener. With music, he was taking her on a romantic journey with him to green rolling hills, to moonlight, to tender moments filled with kisses and caresses. To a lovers' world.

On the last note, applause resounded in the room. Meg felt as if they were alone. She knew Sean returned to the table, thanked Ryan and took the flute, but she was lost in the memory of the gentle, romantic notes. They drifted around in her mind. As sounds in the room became louder, her memory captured the moment. She stared at the smiling blue eyes across the table. Even as she forced herself to return to her surroundings—to hear once more the noise of buzzing conversation, raucous laughter and silverware clicking against plates—she knew she'd never forget the moment. Tenuously, she slipped her control back in place. But it was very flimsy control, Meg realized.

Ryan reached across the table and touched the wisps of hair brushing her brow. "Do you know the name of the song?"

Meg struggled not to react to his touch. "The Kerry Dance."

"Do you know the words to the song?"

She knew the words well.

"It's about sharing one night of madness."

Meg drew a deep breath, but nothing helped her ignore the soft seduction in his tone. It floated over her like a caress. "Madness" would definitely be an accurate description if she were to allow herself to share passion with him. She had to remember that. But she'd never met a man who possessed such contradictory characteristics. He was tough and sensitive. One moment she felt relaxed with him as if he were an old friend, and then the next moment he sparked something within her that made her feel that a chemistry existed between them. "It's a lovely song," Meg managed. "But one night of madness sounds to me like a one-night stand."

Her bluntness stirred his laughter. "Don't you have any romance in your heart, Meg Gallagher?"

"Yes. But," she added, shaking her head and trying desperately to lighten the mood, "not for one night of madness."

Ryan remained quiet for a moment. He remembered staring at her photograph nearly two years before, feeling a certainty about her that had nothing to do with simple admiration for a beautiful woman. He'd wanted to meet her then, learn more about the woman who'd volunteered to baby-sit five nieces and nephews under the age of six, who'd been first in her self-defense class, who'd wanted to do police work. She'd been too interesting to resist. Then Jim had told him that she was engaged. Ryan hadn't been surprised. She was the kind of woman a lot of men would be attracted to. But she'd placed certain men on an ineligible list. "You mean not for a cop." He saw vulnerability flash in her eyes. He didn't want to hurt her, but he couldn't keep skirting the real problem between them and make any progress. "Jim told me about Kevin. It was a difficult time for you."

Meg stared down at her plate. Gratefully, she no longer felt the pain from the loss. She'd come to terms with it, accepted that she had to go on. "Yes," she said more easily than she expected. "I was like a lot of women are. I didn't face reality about the job he'd chosen. About the danger. It was difficult. Probably because I wasn't prepared for the life-and-death occupation he'd chosen."

Ryan looked down and tightened his jaw. There were a lot of different kinds of cops. Words clung to the tip of his tongue. Words about Kevin Duran that Ryan knew he couldn't say to her.

"I never thought about the real danger," Meg admitted. "My dad had the same job to do, one he loved. But I know now my family shielded me from the reality of that job. I really didn't realize the danger existed. I knew it did," she tried to explain. "But I believed *that* happened to other people." Understanding warmed the cool blue of his eyes. The look forced Meg to take a long breath for control. "At the time I was stunned. Kevin was a good cop. He'd been on the force less than a year and had nearly received a commendation for saving a woman from a burning car. That didn't surprise me. He acted on impulse, wanted to help people whenever he could. That was why he became a cop. And he wanted to be a good one. He hadn't just taken a job for the steady income and the pension plan. He was ambitious. He wanted to be known as one of the best." She gave her shoulder an imperceptible shrug. "But no matter how good he was, that didn't save him."

"A lot of jobs carry risks."

"I'm aware of that. That's why I'm choosing more wisely."

"You think you can choose who you fall in love with?" he asked. He knew damn well he hadn't been able to make that choice. Somehow it had been made for him— she was the one. Whether she wanted him or not, she was the one who awakened every tender emotion he possessed.

"Of course, it's not that simple."

Ryan released a mirthless laugh. "You're damn right it isn't."

Meg met his intense gaze, certain he'd been on a school debating team.

"You like mysteries."

Meg nodded, wondering if her brother had also told him that she had a raspberry birthmark on her left hip. Meg gave him a weak smile. "I never realized what a motor mouth my brother was."

Ryan returned the smile. "No, I'm nosy. Asking questions also goes with the job."

"I love them," Meg admitted. "As a kid, I devoured Nancy Drew books. Later, Dashiell Hammett." Her eyes brightened with enthusiasm. "That's why I couldn't walk away from law enforcement completely. And investigating doesn't contain the same kind of danger. Jim spends most of his time on missing persons and insurance claims. My brother Patrick is a lawyer, and my other brother Brian is a probation officer. My dad's retired now and away from that uncertainty. I just don't want that in my life again."

"So you date men like Elliott."

Meg set down her fork again. Her brother needed some lessons on keeping his mouth shut. "I date him occasionally. And the only danger he faces is getting bit by a rabbit that he's pulled out of a hat. I lost one man that I love. I don't want to lose again.''

Ryan kept his voice calm. ''Well, looking for the right person is like solving a mystery. The person you're really after might not be the one you're expecting him to be.''

His logic made her smile, but Meg stood firm in her beliefs. ''In Albuquerque, what division are you with?''

''Homicide.''

''That's not a management or technical-service division,'' she pointed out.

Ryan said nothing. The firm set of her lips announced a stubborn streak. After her dodging him for over a week, he saw no gain in arguing further with her. He wanted to be with her. At the moment, she willingly accepted his company. And for this moment, he'd accept that.

Meg took a sip of water, contemplating her next question. A blunt question which her curiosity refused to forget. ''What happened with your *live-in*?''

Ryan smiled over the term she'd used. He liked her no-nonsense attitude. He'd noticed that about her from the first moment, when she'd held the gun in her hands. She would make a good investigator. She wanted answers, whether she had a right to them or not. ''We decided to see if we'd live compatibly together. We found out we couldn't.'' He watched her brows knit in a concerned expression.

''I'm sorry for prying.''

''I'm not mourning a lost love. I was working on the police force then. And she couldn't handle a cop's life.'' He saw her understanding look, and discerned what she was thinking. But before she had a chance to reiterate her convictions, he added, ''It's not what you're thinking.

She didn't like the hours, the changing shifts, the need I felt to help people."

"And you didn't want to do a different kind of work."

"Not for her. No," he said firmly. "If she couldn't understand why I got involved, then I figured she really didn't understand me."

Meg smiled. "One time my mom said that a policeman is never off duty. The woman he marries needs to realize that."

Ryan looked down at the beer in his glass. He suddenly felt that the wall between them wasn't quite so impenetrable. "You said that your dad is retired now?"

"Uh-huh. They bought a home out of the city. They really like the country living." She sent him an inquiring look. "Do you have family in Albuquerque?"

"No." Ryan shook his head. "My father died when I was younger, my mother five years ago." He watched a small crease form a line between her brows. "My stepfather is in Florida now. One sister lives in California, and the other is in Wisconsin."

His family seemed scattered, yet the warmth in his voice told her that they weren't any less close-knit than her own. "Who taught you to play the flute?"

"My father," he answered, pleased by her interest. His voice softened with a fond memory. "He loved to read poetry and tell Irish fables, and he filled the house with music. He was born in Killarney and came to America when he was ten. He was eighteen when he met my mother. I've been told it was love at first sight." His eyes smiled. "I was also told that he won her over by playing love songs on his flute."

"A romantic soul."

Dimples cut deeper into his cheeks. "A cop."

A smile played across her lips. "I thought that policemen are taught to deal in facts. Your father was one, yet he believed in love at first sight?"

"To him, that was a fact." Her skeptical look made him laugh. "I'll give you this, Meg. You try hard."

She looked up in puzzlement. "Try hard? At what?"

"To veil your romantic nature."

Meg held tightly to her composure. She struggled to keep her voice airy, to make light of his words. "You seem to have an overabundantly romantic one. You believe in love at first sight, don't you?"

"Absolutely."

His eyes met hers with a directness that rocked her. With that one calmly said word, he seemed to pull her fractionally closer. After all the teasing remarks, why did he have to look so deadly serious now? Meg shifted uncomfortably on the chair as her breathing turned unsteady. She lowered her head and began hunting in her purse for her wallet. She needed to get away from him. She had to, she realized, aware of a growing need beginning to build within her. A need that made her want to believe him.

Ryan frowned over her desperate search. She was ready to fly from him. He was used to gauging situations, had learned through trial and error when to rush and when to slow his pace. Watching a mixture of expressions cross her face, he sensed the conflict warring inside her. He didn't want her running from him. Back off, he told himself. At least a little. Biding his time came naturally. Hundreds of stakeouts had taught him the importance of waiting. As she reached for her blazer, he peered hard at her. "I've been sitting here dying of curiosity."

Meg stilled and looked up at him. He smiled; she calmed. Her own reaction amazed her. What was it about him that affected her so? "About what?"

"About this."

Unexpectedly, he reached across the table and brushed a finger across the black script letters of her name above the pocket of her yellow bowling shirt. Meg's breath caught in her throat. Though he hadn't actually touched her, his action wasn't casual. Deliberately, he'd made a move. First he'd lulled, then he'd thrilled her. Meg narrowed her eyes, wondering if she was up to the challenge he presented. She rarely did anything that she didn't want to do. And she didn't want to get involved with him. But she sensed he was used to getting what he wanted. At the moment, he seemed to want time with her.

He twirled a finger in the air. "Turn around. Let me see the back."

Meg complied with his request. "O'Hegarty Imports sponsors our bowling team," she said. Quickly she grabbed a few calming breaths before turning to face him again. "I've worked as a clerk in the store every summer since I was sixteen and part-time now while I finish college."

"That's where you were working before you offered to help out Jim?"

Determined to take control of the situation, she pushed back her chair. "With exams coming up, I was only working a couple of days a week, so I wasn't leaving him shorthanded when I decided to quit and help Jim."

As he stood beside her and helped her with her coat, Meg said before he had a chance to offer, "I have a ride. I drove here," she added, confident she *did* have control, since she wouldn't have to rely on him for transportation home.

"I'll follow you home in my car."

His request seemed simple enough. Meg nodded agreeably as he followed her toward the cashier. "The car is still running?" she asked, amazed as an image of the green dented car with its missing hubcap came to mind. She glanced over her shoulder to see if she'd offended him.

His brow lifted slightly, but he grinned. "I suppose some people might view it as a jalopy. But it's not."

Meg restrained a smile at his serious expression. "It's not?"

"No. It's a Studebaker 'Bullet Nose.' A classic vehicle. It just needs a little fix-up."

Meg stopped at the cashier's counter. "If you say so."

"Yeah," he answered in the same deadly serious tone. "She just needs some sprucing up."

Why did all men refer to their cars as she? Meg wondered. She met him at the doors and then stepped outside. Briefly, her eyes scanned the street. "Where are you parked?"

Ryan pointed. "Right over there, by the corner."

Meg skeptically eyed his vehicle. "Are you really going to restore *that* car?"

"When I get a chance." He slipped a hand under her elbow and urged her toward her own car. "They're going to have some real classics at the auto show. I was there waiting for Elizabeth Howard," he explained.

Meg's head snapped up. "Has something new happened?"

"No, I checked out a few models who might have lost the job she got."

"Did you learn anything?" she questioned.

"None of them seemed upset. Most of them have landed other assignments. A few of the models ended up getting jobs at the show."

"The show doesn't start for a while. Does it?"

"No, but the coordinator's already been working with the models. And some of the displayers were there today. One guy, an Irishman from Chicago named Sullivan," he said on a grin, "is going to display a 1935 Packard. Mint condition."

The pleasure in his expression surprised her. It was boyish, excited. She sensed that his interest surpassed simple enjoyment.

"Vintage-car owners love to talk," he told her.

"Did anyone ask why you were there?"

Her question was a good one. Having a good cover was important. And she realized that. Ryan gave a quick shake of his head. "Everybody was busy. But Sullivan asked who I was and then talked to me for twenty minutes straight."

Meg sent him a puzzled look. "Why?"

"I told him that I was with a magazine. He probably thinks he'll get a big write-up," Ryan said on a laugh.

"Was he interesting?"

The look he gave her answered her without his saying a word.

"One of the displayers I talked to was interesting. Ed Brey. He's from Cleveland. He told me when his dad was alive, they had a '56 Thunderbird in their showroom. A '56 Thunderbird was the first car I ever restored," he said on a sentimental note. As she looked up at him, he saw her eyes. They sparkled with a smile. "What's so amusing?"

"You. It sounds as if the job is proving to have some rewards for you."

"Since Elizabeth has a modeling job at the show, I have a good reason to be there." Ryan gave her an embarrassed shrug of a shoulder. "My dad hooked me on classic cars. One Christmas he bought this expensive car kit. We finished putting that 1929 Duesenberg together right before he died. I have some good memories every time I see one."

"And so when you got older, you started restoring the old vehicles?"

"Uh-huh."

"Is it considered a lost art?"

He chuckled. "No, nothing like that. A lot of people restore them."

Meg nodded while instinctively hunching her shoulders together. The night air whipped through her clothing. She raised her face and threw her head back as the wind tossed her hair.

"Are you cold?" Ryan asked but didn't wait for an answer. He moved close, taking hold of the lapels of her jacket. As he pulled them together, instinct urged him to draw her closer. He considered his actions for a moment. Only a moment. Standing beneath the streetlights, he watched shadows dance across her features. He stared into luminous-looking eyes and forgot his good intentions to move slowly with her. His eyes flicked to her lips. "Did you know that there are a lot of lost arts?"

As he continued to grip the lapels, Meg warned herself. Step back. You don't want him to hold you. You especially don't want him to kiss you. Talking with him had been too easy. Liking him was too easy. "Really?" she answered, starting to draw away, but he held firm. "Like what?"

"Spooning." He grinned as he used the antiquated term.

His answer threw her off balance. An amused smile tugged at the corners of her lips. "Necking?"

"Uh-huh. It's a lost art." Briefly, his gaze returned to hers and then drifted back to her mouth. "No one takes the time for it anymore."

Meg nervously nibbled on her bottom lip. "I wouldn't know."

"Believe me," Ryan assured her. With the darkness around them, her teeth looked like pearls. Her lips tightened nervously then relaxed as if inviting. "Today, people don't want to take the time. It's a look across a room, your place or mine, and bed. No time for . . . kissing, caressing, loving," he finished on a whisper. "Seems a shame, doesn't it? That something that enjoyable is being forgotten."

Meg felt her legs weakening, threatening to sway her against him. Like a strong, gripping magnet, the sensual pull kept tugging at her, urging her closer. Resisting it made her feel breathless, drained. As her body began to relax beneath his touch, she sensed she wasn't going to be able to resist him. Before dating Kevin, she hadn't ever felt that any man had control over her. Even he hadn't. They'd had a sensible relationship based on common interests. Eventually, they'd grown more serious about each other. The next natural thing to do had been to talk about getting married. The relationship had developed slowly, sensibly. There was nothing slow or sensible about what she felt when Ryan was near. Feelings rippled like wildfire through her. Tingles that thrilled swept down her body. She felt heart-stopping excitement. Pure and simple excitement. She wanted to tell herself that what she was feeling was absurd. Chemistry? That notion seemed ridiculous, too. But she wondered if they'd naturally blend or turbulently mix with each other just as chemicals did. Were some people meant to make sparks? It's like an experiment. Just an experiment, she thought as he leaned closer, bending his head toward her. Her lashes flickered as she anticipated his kiss. She wanted it, she realized, tilting her head slightly, bringing her lips a hairbreadth from his.

Then his mouth met hers.

His lips teased, brushing the corners and nibbling gently until she parted her lips. And as the pressure increased, she realized that some experiments explode.

His kiss burst heat within her. It bubbled through her veins, feeling as if it needed only a moment longer to turn into an uncontrollable blaze. She'd known passion's fire before, but had always managed to douse it. For an instant of a moment, she considered letting the vibrant warmth run rampant through her. That moment was brief. Before the mixture had a chance to stir and create something she had no idea how to control, she started to resist. But the power of his kiss took over. Persuaded. Seduced. She realized that chemistry was too logical, too scientific to explain what she was feeling. This was magic.

He practiced sorcery. Like a wizard, he bewitched and weaved a spell. Meg trembled beneath it, feeling as if he had control of both of them. Stunned and bewildered, she clung to his jacket, needing something solid to hang on to.

His shoulders provided that support. Beneath her fingers, she felt the soft texture of his jacket. But she felt more. The heat of his body flowed into her fingers and seemed to follow a slow but steady path through her body. Warmth filled her as his tongue met and dueled with hers. Invaded. Using a kiss as his only weapon, he conquered, weakening in her any thought of battling him. With the quick efficiency of a well-trained strategist, he made his conquest. Though he took only the kiss, he wielded the power of a seduction.

Seconds passed before she acknowledged that he'd lifted his head. Meg snapped herself from a dazed state. Fury raced through her. Fury with herself. He's a policeman. How could she have forgotten that? How could she have let the persuasiveness of his kiss overshadow the heartache she'd felt when Kevin had died? Never again. She never wanted to experience that pain of loving and losing again, she reminded herself, jerking away to pull free from his grip. "Why did you do that?"

"I wanted to."

"Ryan..." Meg started, determined to stop anything between them before it became something. He placed a fingertip on her lips. The warmth of his flesh surprised and silenced her.

"I told you. I believe in love at first sight."

"With me?"

He raised an answering brow.

"That's crazy," Meg said breathlessly.

"Could be," he said, slipping her car keys out of her hand and turning away to unlock her car door. "But that's the way it is."

"It can't be."

Ryan faced her and set her keys on her palm. "Why? Because you don't like me?"

"No...no, it's not that."

"Then what?"

"I don't want to get involved with you. Ever," Meg insisted.

Ryan smiled broadly and touched the small of her back, urging her into the car. "Ever is a long time, Meg," he said before he closed the car door for her.

Meg stared into her rearview mirror as he walked toward his car. Too vividly she remembered the feelings that had pumped through her when they'd stood beneath the streetlight.

Damn, she thought, frowning as she realized the impact his kiss was having on her. Why? Why did she feel this way about *this* man? If she gave into the attraction... No, she couldn't. Unhappiness would follow. She couldn't allow herself to fall in love with him. All they could possibly have was a dead-end relationship. Her shoulders sagged with the thoughts. She wished that he'd never kissed her.

Chapter Six

A sliver of a moon peeked out from behind quick-moving clouds. Sitting at the kitchen table, Meg stared out the window at the sky. A turbulent-looking sky. Everything seemed in a turmoil, she thought, feeling as restless as she had fifteen minutes before when she'd decided to pour herself a glass of milk. People don't fall in love at first sight, she thought for the hundredth time in the past two days. Cradling the milk glass, she wondered what had made Ryan make such a ridiculous statement. They hardly knew each other.

At the rap on the back door, she nearly bolted from the chair. Through the sheer curtain covering the glass in the door, she saw Ryan. Act casual, pretend the conversation never existed, she told herself as she walked toward the door. Casual. Casual, Meg repeated and swung the back door open. Her eyes widened at the sight before her. She knew she was gaping but couldn't stop herself. "What in the world happened to you?"

Mud coated his hair and clothes. Though he'd wiped the muck from his hands and face, the mire glued together the hairs of one eyebrow. She felt an incredible urge to touch it and made herself step back to hold the door open for him.

Ryan gave her a wry grin. "I promise you, I haven't been making mud pies."

Glancing down, Ryan saw the mud clumped on the soles of his sneakers. Mentally muttering a curse, he slipped out of his shoes before striding into the kitchen in his stockinged feet. "Elizabeth and I fell into a mud puddle."

"You and—you and Elizabeth," Meg stuttered, feeling an unexpected wave of jealousy ripple through her. She had no right to be jealous, she reminded herself. But she felt the emotion anyway. Elizabeth Howard was a beautiful redhead. Tall and willowy. Meg thought she was a little scatterbrained, but if a man didn't care about intelligence, she'd appeal to him. "What are you talking about?"

"I was walking with her when someone lost control of his car. I pushed her out of the way, and we both landed in a puddle. Not a clean puddle," he added, showing an irritation she'd never witnessed before. "Oh, no. In this whole concrete jungle, we have to land in the one puddle that's near a construction site."

Meg turned away and headed toward the stove while stifling a smile. Though the situation was serious, his exasperation seemed so out of character for someone usually so calm, so controlled. "Would you like a...?" Her words trailed off and she whipped around, the implication of what had happened settling in on her. "Was it deliberate?"

Ryan slipped out of his mud-soaked jacket and hung it on the back of a chair. Facing her, he began to roll up the sleeves of his shirt. Though the pin-striped shirt was clean, the cuffs were wet and dirt-spotted. "There's no way to know that."

Meg kept her eyes on his as she moved closer. Eyes didn't lie. She'd always believed that. "Was Elizabeth hurt?"

Ryan shook his head. "No."

"And you?" she asked although she'd already scanned his body in a thorough quest for visible injuries.

He bent his head to complete rolling up the cuff. "I'm fine, too. We both just got slopped."

Meg stood inches from him. The hard thud of her heart announced the concern she felt for him. Concern she didn't dare reveal to him. "What do you think? Do you think it was deliberate?"

As she tipped her head to see his face better, Ryan felt her insistence for eye contact. He met her eyes. They reminded him of violets, deep purplish-blue violets. The flicker of emotion he saw in them assured him she wasn't indifferent to him. Inwardly he relaxed. For the past two days, he'd considered his own actions the other night. He came up with the same answer all the time. He'd acted stupidly. He'd meant to move slowly with Meg. Instead, he'd made an announcement that probably had convinced her he needed a straitjacket and a padded cell. Before he'd ever arrived in Chicago, he'd known her feelings about not wanting to get involved with a cop again. Jim had warned him that she'd be wary even if she liked him. But he'd been overconfident. As a cop, he knew better. Overconfidence often meant disaster. "It's possible," he finally answered. "But whoever has been bothering her, he hadn't done anything violent before."

94 PERFECT PARTNERS
Meg turned away with a frown. His answer seemed evasive. He was trained to see things most people didn't. "Would you like a cup of coffee?"

"Coffee?"

Meg kept her back to him, certain that if she faced him, she would see that knowing grin of his. "It seemed silly not to have some in the house. My father drinks coffee."

Ryan held down a smile. "That's a good reason to buy it."

Meg listened, waiting for the chair to scrape on the floor tile. When she knew he was sitting, she turned around to bring him the cup. "Did the car stop?"

He looked up at her. "No."

"So it could have been hit-and-run?" she asked, standing before him with the cup cradled in her hands.

"Could have been."

"And it also could have been deliberate?"

"I think so."

Meg set the cup before him and quickly sat down on the chair next to his. "You didn't tell Elizabeth that?"

"Hell, no. I made light of the whole incident."

Meg nodded. "That's good. She's so frightened." Meg frowned at the liquid in his cup as she remembered how panicky Elizabeth had seemed the last time Meg had seen her. Despite Ryan's agreement about working together as partners, Meg had continued to work alone to avoid spending too much time with him.

Wanting to tie up loose ends about Elizabeth's previous boyfriends, Meg had gone to Elizabeth's apartment the previous morning. The woman had paced the whole time that Meg had talked to her.

Ryan brushed a knuckle across her cheek to get her attention. "You act surprised that she's so frightened."

She moved her shoulders, trying not to think about the way her pulse pounded with his caress. "The man hasn't made a threat. Until now," she added. "If that was him in the car. And until now, he's acted like a prankster. So why is she so frightened?"

"She's a jittery woman."

Meg made a face. "What a term."

"She is one."

"Why is she?"

"I don't know."

Meg watched his eyes narrow in a deciphering manner over the rim of the coffee cup. The moment they did, she knew that he wasn't thinking about Elizabeth anymore. She tensed, waiting, sensing that the question in his mind was going to back her into a corner.

"I don't think you should do any of the investigating by yourself anymore," Ryan said firmly. "We really don't know if this incident tonight was deliberate or not."

"Do you think it's possible she's imagining everything?" Meg asked. At his questioning look, she explained her previous comment. "Except for claims about the phone calls and her tires being slashed, there's no evidence of anyone bothering her. Even the car nearly hitting you two tonight might be unrelated."

Ryan shrugged a shoulder. "I guess that's possible. But she hired your brother to do a job. And we've got that job now."

Meg stared thoughtfully at the milk in her glass. He was right. Regardless of what she thought, Gallagher Investigation Service had been hired to do a job. "Yes." Meg nodded agreeably. "But we'll get more accomplished if we work separately but keep each other informed."

"I don't think it's a good idea."

As he rested his forearms on the table and hunched forward, Meg leaned back on the chair. "I do."

"Jim doesn't."

Meg stiffened her back. "I do."

He released an exasperated sigh. "In other words, nothing Jim or I say is going to make any difference?"

Meg sent him a sweet smile. "I don't know why that should be a problem. Why shouldn't I work alone on this? You're obviously doing the same thing."

His puzzled look annoyed her.

"You were with Elizabeth today, weren't you? On business?" A smile flashed into his eyes, making Meg want to bite her tongue off for asking the question.

"She called."

"She did."

"Uh-huh." Ryan grinned more widely, enjoying himself. He grabbed his cup to finish his coffee. "She had to go for a dress fitting for the auto show. She wanted someone to go with her because her appointment was at night." He looked down at his splashed Levi's. "So I went with her and got a free mud bath." He laughed softly and pushed out of the chair. "What a mess. I guess I'd better get cleaned up."

Meg nodded, deciding her best course of action meant keeping her mouth shut.

As Ryan reached the door, he looked back at her. "Did you think I had a personal interest in Elizabeth?"

Meg didn't glance back. She shrugged her shoulders. "That's none of my business. But as my brother said, she is a knockout."

"Yes, she is. But then so are you. And *you* make great coffee."

SILHOUETTE

 PRESENTS

A
Real Sweetheart
of a Deal!

**PEEL BACK
THIS CARD
AND SEE
WHAT YOU
CAN GET!
THEN...**

Complete the Hand Inside →

*It's easy! To play your cards right,
just match this card with the cards
inside.*

Turn over for more details . . .

Incredible isn't it? Deal yourself in __right now__ and get 7 fabulous gifts. ABSOLUTELY FREE.

1. 4 BRAND NEW SILHOUETTE ROMANCE NOVELS – FREE!
Sit back and enjoy the excitement, romance and thrills of four fantastic novels. You'll receive them as part of this winning streak!

2. A BEAUTIFUL AND PRACTICAL PEN AND WATCH – FREE!
This watch with its leather strap and digital read-out certainly looks elegant – but it is also extremely practical. Its quartz crystal movement keeps precision time! And the pen with its slim good looks will make writing a pleasure.

3. AN EXCITING MYSTERY BONUS – FREE!
And still your luck holds! You'll also receive a special mystery bonus. You'll be thrilled with this surprise gift. It will be the source of many compliments as well as a useful and attractive addition to your home.

PLUS

THERE'S MORE. THE DECK IS STACKED IN YOUR FAVOR. HERE ARE THREE MORE WINNING POINTS. YOU'LL ALSO RECEIVE:

4. A MONTHLY NEWSLETTER – FREE!
It's "Heart to Heart" – the insider's privileged look at our most popular writers, upcoming books and even recipes from your favorite authors.

5. CONVENIENT HOME DELIVERY
Imagine how you'll enjoy having the chance to preview the romantic adventures of our Silhouette heroines in the convenience of your own home! Here's how it works. Every month we'll deliver 6 new books right to your door. There's no obligation and if you decide to keep them, they'll be yours for only $1.95! And there's no extra charge for postage and handling.

6. MORE GIFTS FROM TIME TO TIME – FREE!
It's easy to see why you have the winning hand. In addition to all the other special deals available only to our home subscribers, you can look forward to additional free gifts throughout the year.

SO DEAL YOURSELF IN – YOU CAN'T HELP BUT WIN!

You'll Fall In Love
With This Sweetheart Deal
From Silhouette!

SILHOUETTE BOOKS
FREE OFFER CARD

PLACE
YOUR
WINNING
CARD
HERE!

4 FREE BOOKS • **DIGITAL WATCH AND MATCHING PEN**
• **FREE MYSTERY BONUS** • **INSIDER'S NEWSLETTER** •
HOME DELIVERY • **MORE SURPRISE GIFTS**

☐ *YES! Deal me in. Please send me four free Silhouette Romance novels, the pen and watch and my free mystery gift as explained on the opposite page.*
215 CIL HAXC

First Name	Last Name

PLEASE PRINT

Address		Apt.

City	State

Zip Code

Offer limited to one per household and not valid for present subscribers. Prices subject to change.

SILHOUETTE NO RISK GUARANTEE

- There is no obligation to buy – the free books and gift remain yours to keep.

- You receive books before they're available in stores.

- You may end your subscription at any time – just let us know.

PRINTED IN U.S.A.

Remember! To win this hand, all you have to do is place your
sticker inside and DETACH AND MAIL THE CARD BELOW.
You'll get four free books, a free pen and watch and a
mystery bonus.
BUT DON'T DELAY! MAIL US YOUR LUCKY CARD TODAY!
If card has been removed write to:
Silhouette, 901 Fuhrmann Blvd.,P.O. Box 9013, Buffalo, N.Y. 14240-9013

By the time Meg turned around, he was gone. Despite her good intentions, Meg smiled, more pleased by his words than she wanted to be.

Determined to face those feelings, Meg headed for Jim's office the next afternoon. If she truly didn't want to get involved with a policeman again, then why was she so afraid to be with Ryan? Her previous actions had seemed cowardly to her, especially for a Gallagher. She didn't have to do anything she didn't want to do. If she didn't want to fall in love with Ryan Brady, then she wouldn't, Meg resolved as she opened the office door.

For a long second, she stood in the doorway and stared at the deli bag on the desk. The smell of corned beef on rye and kosher pickles drifted toward her. Meg drew a deep breath, briefly closing her eyes. She knew who had bought the lunch. The man doesn't play fair, she thought whimsically as she walked toward the desk. Not fair at all, Meg mused as she stared down at the bouquet of violets lying on the desk beside one of two bags. The bag with her name printed across it. The other one simply said Ryan. Meg started to laugh and looked around, wondering where Ryan had gone.

During the next few minutes, she strolled down to the washroom to get water in a vase. When she returned to the office, Ryan still hadn't appeared. Meg stuck the flowers in the water and switched on the telephone answering machine. Two minutes later, she was rushing toward the elevator, responding to a panicky message from Elizabeth Howard.

The trip to Elizabeth's apartment took no more than five minutes. She lived in one of the glass and marble skyscrapers that looked out at Lake Michigan. Meg had been to the penthouse apartment yesterday and a week ago when she'd introduced herself to Elizabeth and had told her that she'd be helping with her brother's cases.

Jim had tagged her correctly, Meg thought not for the first time, as she stared at the woman's striking features. She was a beautiful woman with thick russet hair that fell in waves to her shoulders and framed her expertly made-up oval-shaped face. She stood at her apartment door looking as if she'd stepped out of a fashion magazine, her blue eyes enhanced by a deep shade of lavender eye shadow, her lips a glossy, well-outlined red.

She looked like a woman without a care in the world, but her voice carried an edge of nervous panic as she greeted Meg. "You heard the message I left on your answering machine?"

"Yes." Meg slipped off her leather gloves and stepped forward onto the thick, plush white carpet. "You received a letter?"

Elizabeth nodded and led Meg around an abstract bronze statue and down a step into an all-white living room with a panoramic view of the Chicago skyline. "Mr. Brady is here already."

Ryan turned away from the window and pointed to the paper lying on the table. "Touch only the top right corner. I'll take the paper in and see if I can get it dusted for fingerprints."

Meg sank to the couch as she read the message: Get out of town or next time I won't miss.

Despite Elizabeth's cool exterior, her hand shook as she lighted a cigarette. "I kept hoping the person was just some prankster. But—" she paused, swallowing hard "—this proves he's serious."

Meg shot a worried glance at Ryan. They knew now that someone had tried to hit Elizabeth with the car.

Ryan snuffed out his cigarette in a nearby ashtray. He needed to clear up some questions in his mind. "I've worked from Jim's notes and the information you gave me at our last meeting, Elizabeth. I checked with the agency who handles your assignments here and the one you were with before this in California. You didn't live in California for a long time, did you?"

Elizabeth shook her head. "No. I went there to attend modeling school."

Ryan leaned back against a table. "The director of that modeling school didn't remember any man ever acting love-struck about you or angry at you."

"I told you that I didn't remember any trouble," Elizabeth snapped, then immediately sent him an apologetic look. "I'm sorry. I'm on edge, I guess."

"It's all right," he assured her.

As he smiled, Elizabeth calmed down. Meg understood the Irish charm in his smile. It had the power to brighten the moment and shove aside worried thoughts.

"I checked anyway," he explained. "Sometimes a woman isn't aware of a troublesome male but the people around her are. You told Jim that your last non-modeling job was with Thompson Real Estate as a receptionist?"

Elizabeth nodded. "I did all kinds of odd jobs to put myself through modeling school."

"Like what?" Meg asked.

Elizabeth got up abruptly, almost pacing the room before she walked to the huge window. "All kinds of things that most girls do right after they get out of high school. I worked in a fast-food restaurant, a cleaners, a bank, a photography studio. I did mostly clerical work of some sort or another."

"Not in Los Angeles?" Ryan asked.

Elizabeth faced him. "No. I only worked at the real estate company there. The other jobs were in my hometown."

"Where were you born?"

"Iowa."

"So you had these jobs there?"

"Just the one, at a cleaners. Then my family moved to Ohio." She gave him a weak smile. "A farm girl makes good in the big city," she said, her eyes sweeping the room of the luxury apartment.

"Give me a list of the places you worked."

"Okay," she returned, reaching for a pencil. "But I don't think this will help." She looked up from writing. "I can't imagine you'll make any connection between the man and those jobs."

He sent her a grin meant to relax her. "We'll give it a try anyway. And until we get some idea who we're dealing with, I don't want you leaving this apartment without me."

"Or me," Meg volunteered.

Ryan shot a sharp look of disapproval at her. She ignored him, turning her attention back to Elizabeth. His jaw tightened. He anticipated her balking if he limited her involvement. But he'd be damned if he'd let her get hurt. After waiting years to be with her, he planned now on keeping her safe. Whether she liked his methods or not. "*I'll* be here," Ryan insisted.

Meg fumed at his refusal to let her help. As a woman, she'd be able to accompany Elizabeth to some places that Ryan couldn't go. Meg forced herself to cool her temper quickly; but, determined to help in some way, she set down the paper and suggested, "Why don't we have a handwriting expert look at this?"

"That's not a proven method," Ryan mumbled distractedly while considering the security of Elizabeth's apartment.

"Yes, it is," Meg countered.

Frustration swelled up inside him as she shot an annoyed look at him. He really wasn't against using a graphologist, but his worry for her was mixing with his annoyance over her stubbornness. He returned a sharp glance as he grabbed his jacket from a nearby chair. Meg quickly took the cue and rose from the sofa. She was at the door before he'd slid on his jacket.

"I have a date tomorrow," Elizabeth said in a softer than normal voice. "I really don't want to cancel it."

Meg empathized with her. She looked frightened, afraid to lead a normal life. "That's no problem. We'll go with you."

The woman's dark eyes flicked to Meg. "With me?"

"Near you," Meg assured her, shooting a glance at Ryan to help her explain.

"We'll follow," he added. "Where are you going?"

Elizabeth gave him a weak smile. "A football game. I'm not thrilled over the idea, but my date is a football fanatic."

Ryan nodded. "Okay. What time?"

"He's picking me up at ten tomorrow morning."

"We'll be here," Meg assured her as Elizabeth walked with them to the door.

Ryan touched the small of Meg's back, urging her out the door ahead of him. He held down a smile, wondering if Meg realized she'd instigated a date between them. "Dead-bolt the door." After he heard the double click of the lock, he joined Meg at the elevator.

Impatiently, Meg jabbed a finger at the elevator button. She waited until the doors opened to say what was on her mind. "Graphology is a proven method of investigation. One that we should use."

"In your opinion."

"Yes," she said, preceding him into the elevator, "in my opinion. Yours isn't carved in stone, you know. And even if you say no to having the handwriting checked, I'm still going to do it."

She stared him down. Her pupils darkened, turning almost black, while the blue of her eyes deepened in color. Though he felt as if he were drowning in pools of blue, he saw fire. Imagined the depth of emotion she possessed. The passion she'd reveal to the right man. He wanted to arouse that passion in her. He wanted to kiss her until she stopped being so stubborn. "Do you realize that you have a date with me tomorrow?"

A smile flickered at the corners of her lips. "Yes, I do. Part of our job is keeping an eye on her, isn't it?"

"Oh," he said on a smile. "You're doing it for the job."

"For Elizabeth."

"And you have no objections?"

Meg frowned, trying to concentrate on his words as he moved closer. But her mind kept straying, refusing to hold on to a complete thought. The sound of his voice made her remember his kiss. His smile—everything about him made her remember. Emotion skittered through her. Emotion she wanted to deny. This is nothing special. He's not special, Meg repeated to herself. But she knew she was lying to herself. Heart pounding, she felt weak, drained as if she'd run a marathon. More than anything she wanted him to kiss her again.

Meg struggled to register his actual words in her mind. She shook her head. "None, except that I don't really like football."

He quirked an eyebrow at her. "You don't like football?"

Though she knew his words had been unsensuous, his tone kept swaying her, lulling her as if he were mumbling intimate, persuasive endearments. Meg watched his eyes. Tiny lines formed at the corners as they gleamed with teasing humor. She wanted the tease. She wanted some light bantering. "Baseball," she said, clinging to conversation.

"You like baseball better than football?"

Meg managed to nod her head as his breath suddenly stormed her face. "So do you. You played baseball, didn't you?" she asked as a past conversation with Jim flashed in her mind. "My brother told me that you had a scholarship. A baseball scholarship."

He gave his head a quick nod and then leaned toward her, bringing his face closer to hers.

Her knees trembled from his agonizingly slow movements. Another man would have kissed her by now. Like a cat playing with a mouse, he toyed with her, making her tremble before the pounce. But he wouldn't pounce. He had too much savvy to do that. Experience brought knowledge, patience, smooth finesse. In a low-key manner, Ryan displayed that experience. If she gave him the chance, he'd turn her head with fair words. The Irish in him guaranteed he had a silver tongue. He knew how to tantalize, Meg thought, realizing that with a tilt of her head she'd bring her mouth against his. Was he waiting for that? Did he want her to make the first move? She met his gaze with a steady, firm one.

As if he'd read her mind, he smiled knowingly. His blue eyes smoldered, making her breath quicken. Meg tried to avoid the power of his gaze. She stared at the collar of his light blue shirt. Even that seemed a mistake. She wanted to touch the flesh above the collar, feel the texture of his skin beneath her fingertips. "I saw the violets," she said to break the silence. "They're beautiful."

"The color matches your eyes."

Meg looked up. She had no choice. Her mind refused to think about anything but kissing him. She leaned toward him, felt the gentleness of his hands on her arms as he drew her closer, and she raised her face to meet his.

Her lips met his, but his taste escaped her. The swoosh of the elevator doors opening startled her. Meg jerked back and turned wide eyes on the elderly man staring at them. The man grinned; she blushed. Not even glancing at Ryan, she rushed from the elevator, sending the older gentleman a quick smile before she headed toward the exit.

Ryan's hand reached the door handle first. Meg drew a sharp breath as she preceded him outside. She was driving herself crazy, she thought, disgruntledly. First she wanted him. Then she didn't. She knew she was battling herself, but fear kept nagging at her every time she was with him and kept insisting she pull away.

"Meg." He touched the back of her neck, stilling her.

Her stomach fluttered as his fingertips grazed the sensitive flesh near her earlobe. Instead of a cold touch, his hand felt icy hot against her flesh.

"Where are you going?" Ryan forced himself to put some distance between them. What he wanted to do was close the space, mold her body into his, feel the heat and the passion of her lips beneath his. He prided himself on control, but he was discovering that he didn't have as much as he thought he had.

"The office." Meg drew a deep breath. She knew the danger in familiarity, but something nudged her toward him. "Someone bought me a corned beef on rye."

A tolerant, amused look crinkled the faint lines at the corners of his eyes. "Want company?"

"Yes."

He brushed a fingertip across the tip of her nose. "We're making progress. We finally agree on something."

Meg smiled. He was crazy. Nice crazy, she thought.

Chapter Seven

A brilliant sun teased the mind to believe warmth fluttered on the breeze, but a face-biting, cold wind accompanied the brightness on Saturday morning. Before jumping out of bed, Meg listened to the eight o'clock weather report on the radio. Prepared for a cold day at the football stadium, she dressed warmly but comfortably: a pair of gray corduroys; a white, royal-blue, and black tweed sweater; and a pair of soft leather boots. Though she stepped into the kitchen to make scrambled eggs for breakfast, she felt no hunger. Confusion numbed her. She sat at the kitchen table, trying to make sense of her own feelings. What did she want? Love. She wanted to fall in love. She wanted a family. She wanted what her parents had had—years with someone special.

"I smell coffee."

Meg whipped around in response to Ryan's voice coming from the doorway. She released a quick laugh, a self-conscious one as thoughts about love lingered in her mind. A disturbing flutter swept through her. Annoyed her. She pushed it aside as she headed toward the coffee-pot. "I figured you'd be incoherent until you had a cup," she said, pouring coffee for him.

"So you made it for me? For the sake of the investigation, of course."

"Of course." She thought her answer seemed logical, but his grin belied the simplicity of her words.

"Well, this is for you."

Her eyes widened in surprise at the pineapple he whipped out from behind his back.

"Fresh pineapple in October?"

"From Hawaii."

"Where did you get it?" she asked, moving toward him.

"A few miles from here there's a grocery store that specializes in imports."

"Thank you. I can imagine the traffic you contended with to get this for me."

He shrugged a shoulder. "Bumper-to-bumper traffic is good for the soul. It teaches patience."

She released a husky laugh. "And patience is a virtue."

"So I've been told," Ryan mumbled, certain he was reaching his limit where she was concerned.

Meg handed the cup to him, then turned away to keep busy. She pushed her textbooks to an opposite corner of the table to make room for him. "I hope it's not too strong."

As he took a seat at the kitchen table, she unwittingly followed his movement. Her eyes trailed up his long legs. He was lean at the waist and hips but emanated a wiry strength. Physically, he'd turned her on the day she'd met him. Since then, he'd aroused a lot of other emotions within her.

Ryan tilted his head to read the textbook titles. "Is this what you're studying?" He frowned. "Hematology?"

Meg restrained a smile over his surprised sound. "We're learning how to analyze blood stains."

He shifted toward her, laying an arm on the back of his chair. So relaxed, Meg thought. He sprawls casually in my kitchen chair while my stomach coils into tight little knots.

"What else are you studying?"

"Court proceedings," Meg answered, lifting the scrambled eggs from the frying pan.

"And graphology?"

"No." Meg looked up. "I haven't studied that. But I do know that more than the shapes of letters are analyzed. Experts can tell a lot from line flow and pen pressure, too."

He watched her eyes brighten as she talked about her studies. They were eyes he'd never tire of looking at. Caught up in a second of private enjoyment, he watched the gentle sway of her hips as she walked toward the sink. He wanted to touch her. Her hair, her face, her waist. He wanted the feel of her body beneath him. Strong wants, he realized as he considered how few times he'd even kissed her. He'd felt he had no choice. For her sake, he went slow. But his thoughts, his emotions, his body were in overdrive. As she walked back toward the table with her plate, he cupped a hand around the coffee cup so he wouldn't reach across the table and touch her.

"Well, what do you think?" Meg asked, disturbed by the quietness in the room. "Do you approve of my curriculum?"

Ryan peered at one of the textbook titles. "Is this what everyone takes?"

"Some people want to specialize in other areas like fingerprinting or police photography."

"And do they all eat popcorn while they study?" he asked, smiling as he looked at the huge bowl on the table.

"You found out my secret." She shrugged a shoulder. "I concentrate better if I have popcorn to chew on. I used to pop M & M's but I hated the nickname of Pudge that Jim gave me."

"By the amount of candy I've found in your brother's desk, you'll be able to get even someday."

Meg made a face. "Oh, he'll never get fat. And he didn't start that habit until he decided to try to stop smoking."

Ryan laughed softly and reached into his shirt pocket. "Me, too," he admitted, raising a peppermint stick in the air.

"So you have cravings, too?"

More than you know, Ryan thought.

Opening her napkin, Meg watched him frown. What was he thinking? she wondered, fascinated by the way dimples cut into his cheeks even when he wasn't smiling. She wished he'd kiss her. Eight-thirty in the morning, she thought in amazement, and she wanted him to kiss her. "Are you sure I can't make you something to eat?"

He reached back toward the kitchen counter and then plopped a bakery bag on the kitchen table. "I bought my breakfast."

Meg made a face as he withdrew a sticky chocolate doughnut from the bag. "You're going to eat that for breakfast?"

"Good American fare."

"You're a junk-food addict, aren't you?"

"One of the best."

Meg laughed with him. "A pizza lover, too?"

He tipped his head questioningly and narrowed his eyes. "Don't tell me that you don't like pizza? Everybody likes pizza."

"I like pizza," she assured him.

He released a long breath of relief and then took a good-size bite of the doughnut. "You had me worried there for a moment, Meg."

"Did you think I was an oddball?"

Silence suddenly filled the room. Meg looked up from her plate to find his eyes on her. His look carried a message that belonged in a romantic candlelit restaurant with the soft strains of a violin playing in the background. For a second, she wasn't sitting with him in her grandmother's kitchen. Gone were the raucous sounds of the rock music floating in the air from the radio and the smells of brewed coffee and fried food. A dreamy, romantic haze drifted over her.

"I think you're a very interesting and beautiful woman."

She clung to his words for a long, breathless moment. "Once you told me I was like a kid sister."

He broke the mood, reaching for his coffee cup. Over the rim of the cup, he grinned at her. "You didn't really believe that, did you?"

"You have a convincing manner."

He answered her with a soft masculine chuckle. A nice sound. It was a sound that she realized she'd liked to hear a lot more often.

Seated at Soldier Field one row behind Elizabeth and her date, Meg scanned the field of uniformed players. No female who lived in a house filled with men didn't learn something about football. Meg understood the game. She'd gone to every one of her school matches, but as a cheerleader, she'd usually had her back to the field.

The noise of an anticipating crowd surrounded her, and as the howl of the wind grew louder, she huddled deeper beneath the blanket Ryan had thrown over her shoulders before he'd left for the concession stand. Meg watched as he climbed the stadium steps, a hot dog and a soda in each hand. Beneath the sunlight, his hair glinted a rich mahogany color. She smiled at his look of serious concentration while he balanced the paper cups with skill, dodging an overzealous fan's arms. Around her, the crowd roared, drawing her attention toward the playing field. Meg watched the quarterback drop back to pass. As defensive players closed in on him, he scrambled to the left, then to the right.

A quick grin flashed across Ryan's face at Meg's groan as four defensive players piled on top of the quarterback. "Here you are," he said, sitting beside her. "Just mustard. Right?"

"What did you get on yours?" she asked, peering over his arm at the hot dog he held. He'd smothered the hot dog with condiments. "Everything," Meg said, not waiting for his answer. "I should have known. If all that junk is supposed to make hair grow on your chest, I'm glad I prefer only mustard."

"Only little kids eat a hot dog with only mustard."

Meg deliberately waited until he took a bite. Seizing advantage of his inability to whip back a comment, she defended her preference. "This is the only way to eat them."

"In your opinion," he mumbled.

"In my opinion."

His mouth full, he snorted a laugh. "Your opinion isn't carved in stone, you know."

Meg jabbed an elbow at him for parroting her previous words. "I bet you were a rotten kid."

"I was the best tease at school," he said in a prideful tone.

"I can imagine what you were like. Reddish hair, freckles, boyish grin."

"You're a good guesser."

"Did all the girls hate you?"

"Until I turned eleven."

Meg narrowed her eyes. "Should I ask why they didn't after that?"

"Let's just say I began to appreciate their finer qualities then." His arm slipped beneath the blanket and tightened around her shoulders to pull her closer to him.

Meg instinctively snuggled. Though jackets and jeans placed a barrier between her flesh and his, the heat of his body radiated into her. A pleasurable sensation slipped over her. Too pleasurable, she realized, frowning as she stared at Elizabeth and her date.

At least two inches shorter than Elizabeth, the man had a slight build and shoulders that distinctively drooped. His hair was thinning and he wore wire-framed glasses. Since his looks lacked heart-stopping appeal, Meg assumed that Elizabeth thought he had other admirable traits, such as being the heir to a multimillion-dollar fortune. Meg sipped her soda. The idea of choosing a man because of his wealth would never have occurred to her. How could a woman choose? She stopped her own thought and looked at Ryan, remembering that she'd told him she was choosing wisely who she got involved with. He was right. It wasn't a simple thing to do.

Chicago fans began celebrating by the end of the third quarter. Their team romped over the opposition. Night closed in on the stadium, the air turning frosty as people inched their way down the stadium steps.

In the parking lot, Ryan never took his eyes off the Mercedes that Elizabeth was riding in. Involved in the job of trailing her, he was silent during the ride back to Elizabeth's apartment. When she and her date finally entered the building, Ryan released a huge sigh. Though quiet during the drive home, he shared his thoughts as he turned the car down Meg's street. "Something isn't right about this case. I'm going to make some calls on Monday to Los Angeles and to her hometown in Ohio."

"Do you want me to do anything?"

He glanced away from traffic and smiled at her. "No. Didn't you tell me you had exams coming up?"

"Next week." Meg nodded and glanced at the clock on the dashboard. "I'm glad it's still early. I have studying to do."

A hint of a smile played across his lips. "Worried?"

"Not really," Meg admitted as he braked in front of her house and turned off the ignition. "Just studying a lot," she added, strolling beside him toward the house. "My grandmother had a saying. Too much thinking and not enough doing gets you nowhere."

"Wise woman. I agree with her," he said, moving close behind her as she put the key into the lock. "All talk and no action. Right?"

Meg inwardly tensed as his lips blazed against the side of her neck. Though his hands didn't touch her, she felt trapped by her own wants. A moment passed before she realized he'd misinterpreted her words. "No! That's not what I meant," she insisted, her face whipping toward his.

His hand fanned out on her back and drew her close. Though the movement was brusque and determined, she felt no threat or demand in his touch. "I mean, instead of worrying about exams, I should study for them. That's what she meant. Don't waste time talking about what you're going to do, just…" She watched his lips. Slightly parted, they spoke without saying a word. "Do it," she finished.

An anticipation swept through her. It was like the excited expectation that had filled her as a child on the day before Christmas. She raised her face to his, feeling the same youthful impatience she'd known then.

"I plan to," he returned softly.

Conflicting sensations attacked her senses as he brought his mouth down on hers. She felt hardness. The firm touch of his lips, the iron solidity of his chest, the strength and the power of his body against hers. And she felt softness. His mouth moved sweetly, gently, exploring her mouth. His tongue searched in a questing, subdued manner as if savoring. Meg raised herself on her toes, twined her arms around his neck and pulled his face closer to hers. She'd been kissed hesitantly, gently, passionately before, but she'd never been kissed in such a long, slow, tantalizing way. Power. Excitement. Seduction. The kiss possessed all three. It melted her. When he drew back, she longed to pull his face back to hers.

A warm smile spread from his lips to his eyes. "What happened to your 'never ever'?"

"That wasn't the smartest thing I've ever said."

"Like I said before, we're making progress, Meg."

Expecting him to draw her close again, she was stunned when he started to walk away. "Where are you going?"

"To bed. You have to study, remember?" he said and kept walking.

As he disappeared beyond the shrubbery, Meg stared at the dark stillness for a long moment. Sneaky, devious ... She gave up trying to think of names for him. She only knew that he played havoc with her emotions. Deliberately.

Entering the house, she was aware of a longing that feverishly occupied her body. A bath would help, she decided. And while she soaked in the soothing water, she'd brainwash herself with logic.

The bath helped ease the tenseness in her body, but she continued to wrestle with indecision. She didn't want to stop seeing him. Yet he was a cop. She had no future with him, she reminded herself while slipping on her bathrobe. As she tied the belt, she walked down the stairs. She'd make some popcorn, grab a soda, and settle down at the kitchen table with her books. But would she remember anything she studied? Meg wondered. While she'd sat in the bathtub, she'd remembered the day with him. Would more thoughts about him invade her mind now? Would she again remember his kiss? See his face, his charming smile, his teasing eyes?

Meg gave her head a shake. She had to study. Be firm with yourself, she commanded, flicking on the kitchen wall switch as she stepped into the kitchen. The first thing she saw was the bowl of freshly made popcorn beside her books. She must've left the door unlocked.

Sitting down at the table, she flipped open a book, but her eyes fell, not on words, but on the peppermint stick he'd left there. Meg knew then she'd never free her mind from thoughts of him. She liked his sense of humor. She liked his respect for the workmanship and quality of the older cars. She liked the patience and caring in him that made him nurture dying plants to life. She liked the loyalty and friendship that he revealed with Jim. She liked too much about him. Absently, Meg unwrapped the cellophane from the peppermint stick. What if the emotion was more than ''like''? Could she turn off emotion? Especially one as complicated as love.

Chapter Eight

I have a problem. Come to the guest house.

Meg stood by the back door and continued to stare at the morning note Ryan had tacked to the door. Her stomach knotted with a premonition. Since she'd awakened, he'd intruded on her thoughts as if insisting on forcing her to face her own feelings. She reread the note and acted without further thought, slipping on her parka.

As she strolled across the ground spongy from Sunday night's downpour, she wondered over her own need to see him. Yesterday, she'd deliberately stayed away from the house to avoid him and had spent Sunday with her family. Meg raised her face to bright sunlight. She'd like to blame her ambivalence on the weather. But she didn't lie well, even to herself. So why was she going? It wasn't as if she wanted to see the guest house and make sure he was taking care of it. Usually, she avoided going near it, even when her brother occupied it. Every time she'd seen the shambles that her brother lived in, she'd

teetered between wanting to scream at him to clean up the
mess and feeling a compulsion to do it for him. Ryan
couldn't be worse than Jim, even with his house full of
dead plants.

She drew a deep breath, realizing her mind had been
rambling. She felt nervous and tense. She'd offer a sym-
pathetic ear and understanding words—friendship. She
reminded herself to relax.

Standing a foot away from the door, she smelled bacon and heard a mellow saxophone version of an old
melody. She raised her hand to rap on the door, but it
swung open as if she'd whispered open sesame.

While Ryan had given the impression that he awoke
slowly, he looked incredibly wide awake. Showered,
dressed in a pale blue shirt open at the collar and a pair
of clean dark Levi's, he smiled a greeting.

Meg felt her resolve crumbling. "I got your message."

"Thanks for coming." He held the door open for her
but stood near, narrowing her passing space.

Meg stepped around him and into the house. Immac-
ulate, the two-bedroom bungalow sparkled and gleamed.
Flourishing green plants warmed the atmosphere in the
plain-looking room that contained the kitchen, dining
room and living room. Her brother's beanbag-style sofa
and chair didn't look quite so bizarre. Meg arched a brow
as she faced him. "Very nice." His answering smile
melted her. Too much. In her best down-to-business tone,
she insisted, "So what is your problem?"

"I have bacon made and two eggs ready to be cracked
into a pan," he said, holding them in his palm. "And I
have no one to eat them."

Meg laughed. "Were you expecting company?"

"Hoping for it." Ryan moved toward the stove. "Will you stay?"

"Are you sure it won't be too painful for you to look at them?"

He grimaced. "I'll manage." He tapped an egg on the side of the frying pan. "I still don't know how you can eat them this early."

"I've been programmed to," she admitted. "My mother believes love and food go hand in hand." Meg walked toward the stark white Formica table. On it, he'd set two dark brown place mats, one set of silverware, and two crystal goblets. Meg shot a quizzical look back at him as she sat down. "She was so accustomed to feeding men, she thought I was undereating all the time," she added, noticing that the philodendron that she'd tossed out had the place of honor on his kitchen windowsill. Glossy, bright green leaves stretched on their stems toward the sunlight. "So she kept making things she knew I really liked so I'd eat more."

"Like?"

"Liver and onions and..." The face he made stilled her. "You don't like that either?"

Slowly Ryan shook his head. "What else?" he asked with an edge of hesitation, certain she'd rattle off something disgusting like squid.

"Chocolate cream pie."

He breathed a quick sigh of relief. "That's more like it."

She returned his smile across the table. "Oh, Ryan Brady, you are a junk-food man. Chocolate chip cookies?" she asked speculatively. At his nod, she went on. "Hot dogs, pizza, potato chips, candy..."

"I'll eat any dessert," he answered while sliding the eggs and bacon onto a plate for her. With it in one hand

and coffee for himself in the other, he beamed. "Here you are."

Meg stared at perfectly fried eggs. "For all your protesting, you're not a bad cook, are you?"

"I used to cook for my kid sisters because my mother had to leave early for work."

"Is that why you hate breakfast?"

"Could be, Dr. Freud."

Meg laughed softly and reached for the pepper. As she seasoned her eggs, she glanced up. Her hand stilled as she saw the bottle of champagne in his hand. "What's that for? Are we celebrating something?"

The liquid bubbled as he filled her glass, then his. "Being together."

Meg smiled. "You are a nice man."

Ryan leaned forward and clicked his glass against hers. "*That* is quite an admission."

"Not really. I never doubted that."

His eyes stared at her over the rim of the glass. Though he sat inches from her, his gaze moved over her features with the warm touch of a caress. The moment held a domestic edge, a disturbing intimacy as they sat across the kitchen table from each other, surrounded by his possessions. Meg struggled, as she'd struggled since they'd met. Love didn't overcome all obstacles. She could pretend it would, but she knew in time she'd turn into a shrew, hating his job, wanting him to quit and remove its uncertainty from their life. She couldn't allow her feelings to surface. Cursing her own weakness, she stared down at the plate. She'd eat, thank him for the breakfast, and leave.

"The plant looks healthy," she commented, gesturing with her fork toward the philodendron.

"It needed attention." He flashed a quick grin at her. "Not a bath."

The tease in his voice stirred her smile. "How did you develop this hobby?"

"I was living in Washington when my mother died. When I got to New Mexico, I found her apartment filled with plants. Dying ones." A frown creased a short line between his brows. "I guess because I didn't get home in time for her, I felt obligated to take care of those plants." He smiled wryly. "Now, it's become a challenge. If I see a plant in need of attention, I bring it home and work at keeping it alive."

"Did you know anything about plants when you started?"

"Not a thing," Ryan admitted with a laugh.

Meg looked around the room. "Where did you get all of these?"

"Large discount stores. No one bothers with the plants." His eyes sliced to a corner of the room. "I picked up that African violet yesterday."

Bleached leaves curled downward and brown spots dotted the purple-rose flowers. "What's wrong with it?" Meg asked, genuinely interested.

"Thrips."

"Thrips?"

Ryan chuckled. "Insects that cause the flowers to drop prematurely. The leaves look like that because the plant had too much light. African violets are more of a challenge."

"And you like challenges?"

He grinned at her, his eyes meeting hers with a definite underlying meaning. "All kinds," he assured her.

Meg looked down at her plate. "Are you always successful with them?"

"All they ever need is a little TLC."

She smiled easily. "Tender loving care?"

Ryan nodded. "Best medicine."

"Even for plants?" Meg teased.

"For everyone." He stared at her bent head as she avoided his eyes. Closer, he thought. We're getting closer. "What do you want to do today?"

Meg's eyes snapped up. "What are *we* . . . ?"

"Did you have plans to do something else?"

"Yes," she said. "I plan on raking leaves."

He shrugged a shoulder. "Sounds fine to me."

They worked quietly together in the yard, neither saying a word until they began bundling the leaves in large plastic bags.

Ryan held the bag open while Meg stuffed more leaves into it. "Do you have a few free hours tonight?"

Meg pushed back a strand of hair and looked up at him. "For what? The investigation?"

"A movie."

Meg stared into the bag filled with leaves. They crinkled and snapped as she shoved more on top and pressed her palms down to make more room in the bag. "What kind of movie?"

He released a short laugh. "You pick it."

Meg shot a smile up at him. "You won't like it."

"How do you know?"

"We don't agree about too much."

"That makes life more interesting. You pick it," he repeated, securing a tie around the top of the bag. "Whatever you want to see is fine with me."

"Okay," Meg returned on a lilting voice.

To her surprise, he liked comedies as much as she did. They shared two bags of popcorn through the movie, then spent the rest of the evening rehashing it while playing a game of chess. Even more surprisingly, he ended the evening without kissing her good-night.

During the days that followed, she was busy with school and saw little of Ryan. When they did pass each other in the driveway or at the hospital, he was friendly. Casually friendly. During those days, Meg often wondered if the emotion he'd claimed for her had disappeared. Maybe it never really existed, she warned herself, aware he seemed no longer in pursuit, no longer interested in anything but a friendship.

On the following Tuesday, Meg drove to the auto-show facility. Though the show didn't start until Friday, Elizabeth and the other models periodically had appointments with the coordinator. Knowing Elizabeth had gone for a final dress fitting, Meg expected to find her in a back room with the other models and a seamstress. Instead, Elizabeth sat on a folding chair in the large showroom.

Her shoulders hunched together, her hands tightly clenched, Elizabeth visibly shook as Meg rushed toward her. "What's wrong?"

"Grabbed me. He grabbed me," Elizabeth gasped out.

A tall blond model patted Elizabeth's shoulder. "I was coming out of the fitting room when I saw him grab her and pull her toward the stockroom. When I screamed, he released her."

Meg glanced around. At the far end of the room, workmen busily erected the last of the revolving platforms for the automobiles. One of those men? Meg wondered. An electrician? Or an auto displayer? Was the man even in the room? "Where's Ryan?" she asked, scanning her surroundings again.

"I needed something from my car. He went for it."

Meg nodded and squatted down before Elizabeth. "Did you recognize the man?"

"He grabbed me," she repeated. On the verge of tears, she hiccuped a breath. "He whispered that he was watching me. That he'd keep watching me to make sure I'd leave town."

"Did either of you see his face?"

The blond model shook her head.

Elizabeth's response was the same. "No, I didn't either, but he had on a blue jacket." Her eyes were wide with fear. "He ran down that hall," she said, pointing.

Meg nodded. What now? Deal with the situation, she berated herself and spoke to the model, who was still consolingly patting Elizabeth's shoulder. "Will you stay with her until I get back?"

She nodded. "Of course."

"Stay here," Meg insisted. "Stay in full view of everyone so you're safe. You said he had on a blue jacket?"

"Yes," Elizabeth managed softly.

Meg's thoughts were already on her next action. The hall Elizabeth had pointed toward was empty. But if she hurried, she might catch a sight of the man even if he went out the side exit. She would be able to identify him. She rushed across the huge display room. The corners of her lips curled slightly as she imagined the look on her brother's face and Ryan's if she caught the man. Just thinking about solving the case quickened her stride down the long empty hallway toward the exit.

But her steps slowed as she noticed there were doors on either side of her. Stopping, Meg closed her fingers around the doorknob of the one on the right, and gently she turned the knob. The door didn't budge. Expecting the other door to be locked, too, she was surprised that it wasn't. It squeaked as she slowly opened it and peeked in. Her eyes scanned the maintenance closet swiftly. Closing the door to the empty room, Meg took a deep breath and rushed toward the side exit door.

She saw no one, but a sudden shiver swept down her spine. Nerves! she told herself. A few more feet and she'd reach the door. Once outside, she'd need to take only a few strides to see the parking lot exit. Though she'd wasted valuable time on the hall doors, she knew the congested traffic on the busy street would keep someone trapped for a minute or two in the parking lot. She still had a chance to see his face.

Meg yanked hard on the heavy metal door handle. Nothing happened. Locked. The door was locked.

She whirled around and retraced her steps, the heels of her shoes clicking on the gleaming tile floor. She'd taken only two steps past the hallway doors when her own thoughts froze her to a stop. Perspiration bathed the back of her neck. In a cold sweat, she realized that if someone had gone down this hallway, he too would have been trapped by the locked exit door. Her heart banged against the wall of her chest. She already knew that one of the closet-size rooms was empty. And the other was locked. But couldn't someone have locked it from the inside?

The realization raced a chill up her spine. He had to be in that... The thought hung unfinished in her mind as an arm lashed across her and pulled her back and a masculine hand clamped across her mouth. Hot breath flamed her cheek as a coarse, whispering voice shot angry words at her.

"Tell Elizabeth she'd better leave or else."

Angrily the man pushed her hard toward the wall. Off balance, Meg stumbled and slammed her shoulder against the wall as the man ran from her. She winced, grabbing her throbbing shoulder. Her mind clung to the pain shooting down her arm even as she heard Ryan's voice and running footsteps. A second passed before she realized that he stood before her. She wanted to lay her head on his chest and give in to her shock. But one look at his angry face forced her to put on a brave act. "The man..."

"He's gone," he assured her. He watched her raise her chin a notch. The proud, strong gesture contradicted the look in her blue eyes. Not caring if she rebuffed him, he reached out and pulled her to him. "Meg." He ran a caressing hand over her back. "Damn! What were you doing taking that kind of chance?"

Though his arms remained gentle around her, his voice had hardened. She leaned against the arms tight on her back. "I don't take chances," she countered. "You're the one who does that for a living."

"You don't?" he tossed back angrily. "You talk to me about risks. You don't think what you just did was risky?"

She pushed against his arm and started walking away. "What was I supposed to do? He was near. I might have gotten him. Or seen him."

Ryan caught up with her and grabbed her arm to still her. "What if he'd had a knife or a gun? How would you have protected Elizabeth? Yourself?"

"Elizabeth was safe. I made sure of that."

He watched her back stiffen, sensed the pride and stubbornness rising within her to fight him. He stopped himself from telling her how scared he'd felt for her. He stopped himself from saying more. Later. Later, they were going to have a serious talk. "If you're all right, we'd better get back to Elizabeth."

Meg nodded and moved with him toward the show-room. She didn't feel all right. She'd heard concern in his voice. She expected that. She knew he had a gentle side. But she also heard control. A cold kind of control that reminded her he was a man used to dealing with threatening situations. For a while she'd forgotten that.

Elizabeth seemed calm during the drive to her apartment. Sitting in the back seat, she talked about her financial struggle to get to modeling school.

Meg laid an arm on the back of her seat and shifted on it. Briefly her eyes met Ryan's. He, too, seemed aware of Elizabeth's nervous chatter. Driving, he said nothing, but his brows knitted slightly. It was an expression Meg was becoming familiar with. Unlike her, he hid his emotions well. Though his features rarely offered any clue to his thoughts, his brows did. She'd noticed that they bunched slightly when something didn't seem right to him. Something didn't seem right to her either.

Elizabeth sighed wearily. "The preparations for a show like this are sometimes more tiring than the actual modeling job."

"This isn't the first auto show you've done, is it?" Ryan asked, glancing at her in the rearview mirror.

"No. I worked at one in Detroit. I'd like to do magazine work, but I'm not tall enough for high-fashion modeling."

Though Meg knew Ryan had investigated Elizabeth's background, she asked inconsequential questions to keep the woman from mulling over what had happened. "What do you do besides auto shows?"

"Computers, air travel, boat conventions. I've done a few commercials, too."

"Here?" Ryan asked, annoyed at learning the information so late in the investigation.

"No. In California."

"Modeling must pay well," Meg said, thinking about the luxury apartment Elizabeth lived in.

"Not a lot yet. But I've met some interesting and—" Elizabeth paused "—eligible men who like to share their wealth."

Ryan glanced at Meg. In the dark interior of the car, her features were hidden. But he didn't need to see them to know she was frowning. Her background and her sensitivity never would allow her to place wealth above love if she were looking for a man.

After seeing Elizabeth safely to the door, they headed toward home. A silence filled the air. Meg hesitated for a moment before saying what was on her mind. "For this man to be threatening her life, she must know him. It's impossible for a person not to know if they've angered someone that much." She shifted toward him on the seat. "You told me that there were no fingerprints on the note she got. Is that right?"

Ryan drove the car into the driveway and braked behind Meg's Mustang. He shook his head. "No. No fingerprints on it.

"I had the handwriting checked," she announced, expecting words of opposition from him.

"Okay, Sherlock, what do you know?"

"You're willing to listen?"

He switched off the ignition, shifted toward her and laid an arm across the back of the car seat. "You have a captured audience."

"Why this change of attitude?"

"Because we have nothing. We have no idea who the man is. And we might have a scared, uncooperative client. What's more, I believe anything that can help is worthwhile."

"Why did you act as if you were against the handwriting analysis?"

"The case was becoming dangerous, and I didn't want you getting more involved. I care about you. Haven't I made that clear?"

She felt warm. She could fight the feeling but was enjoying it too much at the moment. She was happy he'd made himself clear about such feelings. Looking down, she reached into her purse and pulled out a slip of paper. "I gave the graphologist this note and he described the man perfectly."

Ryan inclined his head questioningly. In the darkness of the car, Meg saw his eyes sparkle with humor.

"Is that one of my notes?"

"Good job, Sherlock."

He released a deep, rumbling chuckle. "What did he say?"

"He said that the man who wrote *this* note is an enigma."

"An enigma?"

"Uh-huh. Analytical yet romantic and sentimental."

"Do you believe that?"

"Sounded right to me. He also said that the man is generous and quick-witted, has a sense of humor, but..."

He grinned widely. "Of course, there's a but. Knew it sounded too good."

"He said you're controlled and tenacious. You won't give up on something until you get it. True?"

"True."

His eyes sliced to her lips, giving the conversation a different meaning.

"I'm glad you've learned that."

"Ryan, I don't want . . ."

He placed a fingertip on her lips, silencing her. "We're talking about business, aren't we?"

Despite his comment, his fingertip outlined her top lip before he draped his hand back over the steering wheel. No, business wasn't the only thing on his mind. She was sure of that. "So you agree that there's merit in graphology?"

He lifted a brow and nodded. "What did you find out about the writer of Elizabeth's note?"

"The graphologist said that the man who wrote that note to Elizabeth is a thrill seeker. He likes to take chances for fun."

"Would he kill for fun?"

Meg grimaced. "I didn't ask that."

"What else?"

"He has an enormous ego and lives in a fantasy world more than in reality. Though he lacks real confidence, he believes he won't get caught."

His brows knitted. "What if we've been on the wrong track. What if the man isn't angry at her?"

"Isn't angry? Then why would he . . . ?"

"What if the man is feeling threatened for some reason?"

"By Elizabeth?"

"Maybe she knows something about him. And he wants her out of town so he can be sure she won't say anything about him—or see him." He looked at Meg. "It's the only logical thing I can come up with."

"But why wouldn't she tell us?"

"Maybe she doesn't realize she's a threat."

"How could that be?"

"If you see something you shouldn't have," he explained, "that's a good reason for someone to be after you." His frown deepened. "It's possible, too, that she's aware she saw something that she shouldn't have, and she's blocked it out of her memory."

"Like traumatic amnesia?"

Ryan shrugged a shoulder. "Maybe. I don't know."

Meg gave her head a slow shake. "If the man is from her past, why didn't he threaten her before this?"

"I don't know." Ryan chuckled softly. "You keep asking me to give you answers. I don't know any more than you do. I investigated the job she had at a cleaners in Iowa. At sixteen, I doubt that she did anything too earth-shattering to someone. And I can't imagine she saw anything illegal there. So unless someone is carrying a long-lasting grudge because she pressed the creases crooked in his pants, I can't see anyone wanting to threaten her like this."

"And no other leads?"

"Not from that town. The teachers I talked to who remembered her say she was well liked but quiet. I'm going to take a plane to Ohio. Maybe I'll find out something if I talk to people who knew her family, or whom she worked with at those other jobs."

Meg nodded. "And me? What should I do?"

"You could get the list from the auto show of the people who registered with them and find out what hotels they're staying at. And," he added, as if another thought had sprung from nowhere at him, "check on those conventions that Elizabeth finally mentioned to us. See if anything odd happened at one of them while she was working there."

"Okay. Will you be gone long?"

"Just for the day." He smiled at her, wanting to ask her if she'd miss him. He decided against it.

"I hope you get lucky there."

"Even if I don't, we'll find out who he is."

The absolute certainty in his voice conveyed the confidence of a man used to challenges. Used to meeting them. Meg nodded agreeably, sure they'd get the answers.

At the movement of her head, moonlight cast a silver streak across her dark hair. She was near. Too near for him to resist. Lightly, he touched the tips of hair that brushed her shoulder and curled a dark strand of it around one of his fingers. "Earlier you took a damn big chance. No more, Meg," he said so softly that his words came out on a whisper. "Whether you like it or not, we're working together from now on. I insist on that."

"I don't know why you're so angry. I could have been able to identify him," she reminded him. "I might have trapped him. Or caught him."

Ryan shook his head. A flash of anger narrowed his eyes. "As far as this investigation goes, you and I are inseparable. You won't do anything like that by yourself again."

Meg forced herself to keep her voice calm, but she didn't like being told what she could or couldn't do. "And I have no choice?"

"Sure you do. Stay away from Elizabeth."

Meg pushed open the car door and stalked toward the house. Her action seemed childish, but she felt vulnerable. Uncertain. She reached the back door a second before him.

When she slid the key into the lock, his hand captured hers. Her mind cried, don't turn around. But she had to. Her heart hammered in her throat as she looked up at him.

"What are you going to do?" he asked.

· Meg had no reason for anger. She knew he was only trying to protect her. But that seemed to fuel her irritation. His concern was emphasizing the very emotion inside her that she was trying to suppress. "You gave me little choice," she said quietly, even though she wanted to scream. "As you said, you and I are now inseparable."

As she whirled away from him, the wind tousled her hair. Ryan resisted an urge to grab it. Her chin high, her shoulders back, she threw open the door. He winced as it slammed behind her. She may have agreed to his demand, but he wasn't feeling very victorious.

Meg's face showed distaste as she sniffed at the flowers on the bed table beside her brother's bed. Though the vase held a bouquet of flowers, the strong antiseptic smell of the hospital overshadowed their fragrance.

"So you're having trouble," Jim drawled in response to her two-minute tirade about Ryan's chauvinistic, dominating personality.

"He's worse than you and Dad. Everyone thinks I need protecting."

Concentrating on sliding a ruler inside the cast that stretched from his ankle to his thigh, Jim gritted his teeth with a determined expression. The look made Meg smile. A handsome, dark-haired man with brilliant blue eyes, he seemed more boy than man at the moment.

"Damn! This cast is driving me crazy."

"Obviously," Meg said over his pleasurable sigh of relief as he made contact with the itch. His head thrown back against the propped-up pillows, he closed his eyes in a look of peaceful contentment. Meg perched on the bed beside him. "Better?"

"Yeah." He grinned, opening one eye first. "Now, what's your problem?"

"Your good buddy is my problem."

"Because he wants to keep you safe?"

Meg frowned with annoyance. Why did he make it sound so logical? "It's not that simple."

"Well," he said, reaching in back of her and setting the ruler on the nightstand, "I know why we look out for you. We love you." He wrapped a hand around hers. "What do you think Ryan's reason is?"

"He's crazy." She tipped her head questioningly. "Do you know, not a day has passed since he arrived that he doesn't bring home a green plant."

Her brother rolled his eyes and groaned. "He's turning my house into a jungle, isn't he?"

"It looks that way."

"And all those plants are alive and growing," he said with certainty.

"They may be, but he's stifling me. He thinks I'm incapable of taking care of myself."

"Meg, that's not logical. You take care of the house, go to school, spend time doing so many things I can't keep track of them and..." He paused and smiled. "I understand that you've whipped my office into a respectable-looking business. Even my creditors are happier. That doesn't sound like a woman who needs help managing her life."

Jim eyed her for a long moment. Too long. Meg shifted slightly, but she felt like squirming. "Why are you looking at me like that?" she asked on a forced laugh.

"What's been going on between you two?"

"Nothing. We hardly see each other. We..." She clamped her lips together as she realized she was overdoing the denial. "We're working together. Of course, we've seen each other."

"But—" he shook his head proddingly while a smile hovered at the edges of his lips "—other than that, you've hardly seen him?"

Meg avoided his eyes. Staring down at her purse, she fiddled with the strap. The tease in his voice alerted her. He wasn't at all displeased. "He's crazy," she said more softly, in a less excitable voice. She felt her brother's stare.

He'd always been able to pull confidences from her. "He told me that he believed in love at first sight."

Jim squinted at her. "He told you he loved you?"

"No! He told me he believed in love at first sight. With me," Meg added on an embarrassed shrug.

"He does."

Meg's eyes snapped up. "He told you?"

"Yes."

"I told you he's crazy."

"He's crazy about you," Jim said on a laugh.

"You don't find that odd?"

"Nope." He tugged at her hair. "You're a very likable person."

Meg released an exasperated sigh. "Jim, this is serious. I don't want to get involved with him. What's more, we don't agree about anything."

Her brother snickered. "Nothing, huh? You two sound like quite a pair."

Afraid to even think about herself and Ryan as a couple, she flared back impatiently. "We are the most unlikely pair you'd ever meet."

"The lady doth protest too much."

Meg fired a penetrating look at him. "What does that mean?"

Jim grinned. "Nothing, really. But there's a lot of fire in your denial," he added, pushing back to lean against his pillow.

Fire? There was a lot of fire between them. In the few weeks she'd known Ryan, she'd felt more heat with him than she'd ever felt with any other man. Heat? Meg nearly smiled over the word. She had felt the blaze of desire when he'd kissed her. He had melted her with a look, a touch, a kiss.

Her gaze focused again on her brother. As his eyelids drooped with sleep, Meg quietly slipped out of the room so that she wouldn't disturb him. Her life was turning into an unsolvable dilemma because her heart kept ignoring the sensible thoughts in her mind. Meg frowned as she walked toward the hospital elevator. She knew of only one emotion that made sensible people act crazy. Love. Logic and love rarely went hand in hand.

Chapter Nine

Ryan peered through the rain-splattered car window at the people huddled beneath umbrellas, racing through the parking lot toward their cars. Behind a sheet of rain, the buildings of the college were lost to him even though it wasn't dark outside yet. Meg was nearly at the door on the passenger's side of his car before he saw her.

"It's raining so hard that I almost didn't see your car," Meg said as she slipped quickly inside.

"Why didn't you drive your car today?"

"At exam time it's more trouble to get a parking space in this lot than to take a bus. When did you get back from Ohio?" Meg asked, slipping off wet leather gloves and setting them on the floor.

"Early this morning. I guessed you'd already left the house."

"I spent a few hours with Jim before school."

He remained quiet while she set the umbrella on the floor and moved her textbooks from her lap to the seat beside her.

"Did you learn anything in Ohio?"

"First things first," he insisted. She looked tired. That didn't surprise him, but her inexhaustible energy did. She'd seen Jim daily, had studied for exams, and had found time to stay involved in the investigation. "What grades did you get on your exams?"

"An A in Court Proceedings and a B- in Hematology."

"Whiz kid."

"Easy tests," Meg said, stifling a yawn. "Were you with Elizabeth today?" At his nod, she questioned, "Any trouble?"

"She spent most of the day at the modeling agency getting photographs taken for another assignment. And I listened—an audience of one—to her spiel about the car she'll be modeling with at the show. But while she was gone, red paint was thrown at her front door."

"My God. That must have frightened her even more."

"Would you have been frightened?"

As he glanced at her, Meg nodded her head. "A little," she said honestly. "And angry. I don't intimidate well."

"I noticed."

The smile in his voice warmed her. When it came to Ryan, she was on an emotional seesaw. At this moment, she realized, she was teetering toward affection. She wanted only to be with him, enjoy his company.

"You're awfully quiet."

"I was thinking about your trip. Why haven't you told me about it?"

"I got sidetracked," he answered, winking.

Meg pressed her palms against her wet face to dry it. Oh, he did wild things to her with the merest look, she mused, feeling her pulse beat quicken. "So what happened?"

"I went to the places where she'd worked. No one at any of the places remembered any problem. Her family, an aunt, was well thought of, involved with the church and respected."

Meg released a huge sigh. "So, nothing."

"Just the opposite. Elizabeth was a teller at the bank."

Meg nodded, acknowledging that she remembered Elizabeth's mentioning the bank. "She had trouble there?"

"The bank was robbed."

Her eyes brightened. "And she was working there at the time?"

"That's right. The robber walked up to her and demanded money."

"She saw him?" Meg asked, astounded Elizabeth hadn't told them that.

"He wore a scarf."

Meg frowned. "Then why would the man want to get..."

"The scarf slipped. When it did, he threatened her."

"Ryan, why didn't she tell us that?"

"The bank manager told me that Elizabeth claimed she couldn't identify the man."

"But if he was so close..."

"Sure, she could," Ryan confirmed, switching on the ignition and the windshield wipers. "But she told everyone, including the police, that she couldn't identify him."

"But he knows she can." She watched the back-and-forth movement of the wipers. "Why would she say that? She must have realized that the man might come after her." The rain pattered harder on the roof of the car. Meg glanced out the window at the downpour and then looked back at Ryan. Questioningly, she cocked her head. "When you saw her, did she admit to you that there had been a robbery?"

"Yes, she did. But she claimed she never saw the robber's face."

Meg sent him a skeptical look. "If he stood close to her, she must have."

"That's what everyone believed. The bank manager said that the robber pushed the gun barrel against her neck and whispered something before he pulled his scarf back on and left."

"So he threatened her then?"

"And she fainted. When she came to, she acted as if the robbery hadn't happened. In time, with everyone around her forcing her to remember it, she did recall the robbery, but she continued to insist she hadn't seen the robber's face."

"I don't understand. Did she think he wouldn't bother her if she kept her mouth shut?"

Ryan shrugged a shoulder. "She was young and frightened. Frightened enough to quit the job. Within a week, she'd moved to California."

"And the man, of course, believed that he was safe, since he'd never see her again."

Ryan nodded. "Until recently."

"And she really doesn't remember?"

Ryan gave a slow shake of his head. "No, she doesn't."

"Poor Elizabeth. Fear is controlling her life."

His eyes locked with hers. "Fear sometimes makes a person act illogically."

Meg looked out the side window at streams of rain running down the glass. She knew he wasn't talking about Elizabeth's fear. My fear, Meg thought. My fear of falling in love with a policeman again.

"We'll just have to get past that fear," Ryan added, pulling into traffic.

Meg drew a hard breath. She wished she could do that. Life would be easier then. So much easier, she realized. She squeezed her eyes to block out that problem and forced herself to think only about Elizabeth's.

By the time she looked back at him, they were driving past the lake. "I have another idea." Sitting straighter, she prepared for another professional battle with him.

Ryan squinted at the oncoming lights of another car. "What is it?"

"Now, be open-minded," Meg chided. "My graphology idea wasn't a total bust, was it?"

He glanced sidelong at her. "No, it wasn't," he conceded. He released a long sigh. "Let's hear this new idea."

"I have a friend. A very sane friend who is a..." Meg paused, trying to find the right words, convincing ones. "She's a hypnotist." Ryan sent her a look, as if he thought she were crazy. It nettled Meg. "Forget it," she snapped and turned away to look out the window, her lips pressed tightly together.

As she raised her chin a notch, Ryan made a face. He hadn't meant to offend her, but he was from the shoe-leather school of investigation. He believed in tried-and-true methods. "Meg, come on," he soothed. "I didn't mean to upset you."

She swung her gaze back to him. "I'm not upset. But I'd think you'd be willing to try anything to solve this case. We have *no* answers. Do we?"

"No, we don't," Ryan answered grudgingly. He'd checked out the two people who'd been in the small-town bank that day and the security guard who'd been wounded. No one else had seen the robber's face. Annoyed, Ryan knew Meg was right. They'd reached a point of trying anything. "Okay."

"Okay?" she said, surprised.

He glanced away from traffic. "You're right. We've run into enough dead ends. It's time to try anything." At her silence, he shot another glance at her. "If Elizabeth agrees, we'll go see your friend."

"I'm shocked," Meg admitted. "I thought you'd fight me more."

He chuckled low. "Am I that difficult to work with?"

"No, you're easy to work with. But you do stick to more conventional methods."

"And you have a lot of friends who practice hocus-pocus."

"Only Elliott does. This woman is legitimate. Really," Meg assured him as she saw his doubting look.

"Speaking of Zondor the Great, he stopped by the office this morning. What's this craziness about his sawing you in half tomorrow?"

Meg giggled. "I'm assisting in his act."

"You aren't?"

"Yes, I am."

"You aren't going to let him saw you in half?"

"He doesn't really do that. Illusion. It's all illusion," she assured him, mimicking Elliott's dramatic presentation of the word.

"It had better be. By the way, he left your costume."

"Oh. What does it look like?"

Ryan smiled over the excitement in her voice. "I like it. You may not. A string bikini would cover more flesh than the costume will."

Meg groaned. "I'll have to find another one then."

"Why? If you wore it, you'd make Elliott's act a guaranteed success."

"Now, I know I'm going to get another costume." Meg smiled at Ryan's chuckle. As he parked the car outside Elizabeth's apartment building, Meg told him, "Sam has her apartment near here."

"Sam? Her?" Ryan shook his head. "I know this is a mistake."

"Her name is really Samantha."

"And she lives with five cats. Right?"

"She's not weird," Meg insisted. "She lives in a penthouse apartment and makes a lot of money as a..."

Ryan shook his head and held up a halting hand. "Never mind. Don't try to explain. We'll go there. We'll see what happens. But I want a promise from you. If this doesn't work, we don't go to a fortune-teller who looks into a crystal ball to see the future."

He looked so deadly serious that Meg couldn't resist a tease. "What about someone who reads tarot cards?"

He opened his mouth to argue but saw impish lights dancing in her eyes. "Having fun?"

"Yes," she admitted, laughing as he made a face at her.

Though frightened, Elizabeth agreed to go with them. While Meg called Samantha and filled her in on Elizabeth's problem, she heard Ryan talking softly to Elizabeth. His reassuring tone was as magical at calming Elizabeth as his flute playing had been devastating to Meg. He possessed a sensitivity she'd seen her father and brother display, unlike many of the policemen she'd met, who were so cynically hard they'd forgotten how to treat the victim.

By the time Ryan braked the car in front of Samantha's apartment, his soothing manner had Elizabeth almost eager to try anything to end the fear she'd been walking with daily for the previous few weeks.

Samantha Tyler was not what Ryan had expected. Beautiful. Exquisitely beautiful. Soft-spoken with a slight Southern drawl, she greeted Meg with a warm hug, then began talking to Elizabeth.

Their conversation was inconsequential and meant to keep Elizabeth from being anxious. Sitting on a chair opposite the sofa, for a few moments Sam asked questions only about Elizabeth's job. Sam's voice suddenly softened and her words came out slower. "I want you to relax and listen to my voice, Elizabeth. As you listen to my voice, your arms will become very heavy. And your body is getting very tired." Sam's voice never changed its tone. "Your eyes are very heavy, Elizabeth. You can hardly hold your eyes open."

Meg watched, amazed at how quickly and easily Elizabeth was responding to Sam's softly said suggestions.

"Your eyes are beginning to close. Your eyes are very heavy. Your eyes are so heavy that you can't hold them open anymore. I want you to close your eyes and listen to me."

Pleased at the results Sam was getting as Elizabeth's lashes fluttered and then her eyes closed, Meg wondered if Ryan could see Elizabeth's relaxed state from where he was sitting. Meg looked back at him, ready to send him a smug grin. His eyes were starting to close. Meg stifled a laugh as his head bobbed. Immediately, his eyes snapped open. Aware of Meg's stare, he made a face at his own response to Sam's hypnotic tone.

Somehow Meg managed to smother a smile. Proved this one, she thought proudly, turning her attention back to Sam.

"As you listen to my voice, I'm going to take you back in time. Back to the last day that you worked at the bank. Can you hear me, Elizabeth?"

Eyes closed, Elizabeth nodded and answered softly, "Yes."

"Elizabeth tell me what you see?"

As Elizabeth sat still, saying nothing, Meg held her breath. If the hypnosis didn't work, they might never know who she saw that day in the bank.

"It's snowing outside."

"No, Elizabeth. Who do you see in the bank?"

"I see a tall man," she said suddenly, her tone flat sounding. "He's wearing a knit cap and a wool scarf. All I can see are his eyes." She stopped abruptly. Her voice contained an eerie calmness as she said, "And the gun."

Sam spoke in the same monotone. "Forget about the gun, Elizabeth. Tell me about his face."

"Someone moved. He looked away and shot the gun. The security guard is on the floor, blood coming from his leg," she said, tears starting to run from her closed eyes down her cheeks.

"I want you to relax, Elizabeth. Forget about the gun. Forget about the shooting. You don't have to be afraid."

"His scarf is slipping down. Now the gun is against my throat."

"No, Elizabeth," Sam interjected. "Forget about the gun. Tell me about his face. Tell me what he looks like. What does he look like," Sam insisted. "Tell me what you see."

"I see a thin face. Little eyes. And a scar."

"Tell me where the scar is."

"By his lip. A small scar by his top lip."

Sam glanced at Meg. "Do you need more?"

Ryan shook his head. "Not if she could identify him now."

Sam smiled. "There's a good chance that she could. Elizabeth, you did very well," Sam assured her. "Now you are to relax again. At the count of three, I'm going to awaken you and you will feel very refreshed and wide awake. One. You feel very refreshed. Two. You feel wide awake. And three. Wake up."

Elizabeth's eyes opened. Sam waited while she became accustomed to the light in the room. "How do you feel, Elizabeth?"

"I feel fine." She blinked her eyes several times. "Did it work?"

Sam smiled. "You did fine."

"Yeah, you did," Ryan echoed. "You told us what we needed to know. The robber was a tall, thin man with small eyes and a scar at the corner of his mouth."

Elizabeth tensed for a second. "Yes," she said, sounding suddenly winded. "He does look like that." Her eyes darted between the three of them, then settled on Meg.

Despite Ryan's words of encouragement, Meg didn't think a positive identification could be made from Elizabeth's description. Still, she returned Elizabeth's hesitant smile, noting that fear still clouded the woman's eyes.

Meg moved to the sofa cushion beside her. "Elizabeth, don't be afraid. You don't have to be," she said, placing a comforting arm around the woman's shoulder. "We have an idea now about what he looks like. He won't hurt you."

Ryan met Sam's eyes across the room. "Thank you."

"Yes," Meg added. "Thank you, Sam."

"Elizabeth." Ryan pushed himself out of the chair. "If you feel up to it, we should go down to the police station."

Meg looked up at him. "You want her to look through the mug-shot books?"

Ryan nodded. "If she feels up to it."

Elizabeth raised her gaze to him. "Yes," she said without hesitation. "I want to do that."

"Good," Ryan answered. He waited until Meg's gaze met his, then gave his head a barely perceptible jerk, gesturing her to get up.

He walked to the window and stared out at a dark view, lights from skyscrapers barely visible on the rainy night.

Meg joined him by the window. Behind her, she heard Sam speaking in her soft, calm voice to Elizabeth. Meg stopped beside Ryan, touching his forearm. "What did you want?" she asked in a low voice.

"I'm going to drop you off at the office while I take Elizabeth to the police station."

She sent him a quizzical look.

"Go through that list of names of the people registered at the auto show." At Meg's nod, he continued, "Try to verify the names by calling the hotels that they're supposed to have registered at while staying in town."

"What am I looking for?"

"Someone who doesn't exist."

She frowned, puzzled. "You'll tell me later, right?"

Ryan smiled. "Right." He glanced back at Elizabeth. "Now, I'd better get her down to the station."

Two hours passed before Ryan returned to the office. As the door swung open, Meg looked up. "Any luck?"

His hair glistened from the moisture, strands behind his ear determined to curl whichever way they could.

He shook his head and reached forward to slip the pencil out from between Meg's fingers. He set it down, then pulled her chair away from the desk. "We put Elizabeth in front of a computer and brought up Ohio mug shots. No luck. She started looking at federal offenders, but I could tell she was getting too tired, so we left."

"Is she at home now?" Meg asked as he turned away from her.

"No." Ryan grabbed her raincoat off the hook of the coatrack. He held the coat out to her. "I drove Elizabeth to a friend's house in the suburbs."

Meg slid her arms into the coat sleeves. As he stood behind her, she smelled rain on his clothes. Briefly his hands cupped her upper arms and slid slowly up and down them. She wondered if he had any idea what kind of havoc his simplest gesture played on her. He could be dangerous to my health, Meg mused, realizing she'd stopped breathing for a second. She forced herself to pull away from him and reached for her purse.

"She'll be safer there for the weekend," Ryan said. "The police are going to check on her periodically."

"That's good." Meg faced him. His eyes sparkled, assuring her that he knew exactly what his touch did to her.

"Come on, we can talk while I drive."

Meg yawned in response.

"Tired?"

"Hmmm."

"I'm hungry."

Meg glanced at her wristwatch a second before he flicked off the light switch. "No wonder. It's nearly ten o'clock," she informed him as they walked toward the elevator.

"You must be starving," he teased. "Aren't you the lady who eats by the clock?"

As they stepped outside and ran toward his car, dodging raindrops, Meg concentrated on jogging around puddles. Waiting until he had slid behind the steering wheel, she teased back, "I try to. But I have a *partner* who snacks on peppermint sticks and junk food all day." Pointedly she stared at the crumpled potato-chip bag stuffed into the car ashtray.

"I needed energy."

"Me, too," she returned. "My dialing finger is worn out."

"Did you find out anything?" he asked, cautiously pulling out onto the street.

"I'm not sure what I was supposed to be looking for," she said to remind him that he hadn't told her why he'd wanted her to make those calls. "But two men on the list couldn't be found. One of them, a man named John Rachman, was supposed to have registered at a downtown hotel but the hotel manager told me that Rachman had checked out." As Ryan shot a glance at her, she added quickly, "He decided to stay with friends. I didn't verify that yet, but I will."

Ryan stopped for a red light and looked at her. "And the other man?"

"The other man gave the name of an airport motor hotel, but he wasn't registered there."

"Ed Brey," Ryan said knowingly.

Meg peered hard at him. His smile appeared whiter in the dark interior of the car. Unconsciously, she inched her hips closer to him, trying to see his expression better, decipher what he meant. "Yes. How did you know that?"

He concentrated on the traffic as the wind blew rain against the window. "When Elizabeth was under hypnosis, the man she described sounded like Ed Brey to me. Remember I told you about him," he said with a quick glance at her. "I told you that I had talked to a guy from Ohio, whose father had a '56 Thunderbird in his showroom."

Meg nodded, remembering the conversation about the man, about Ryan's interest in vintage cars, about his memories of his father.

"I didn't want to say anything in front of Elizabeth, because I didn't want to alarm her."

"And you're sure he's the right one?"

"Well, you can't find him registered anywhere, and he fits the description Elizabeth gave. A tall, thin man with a scar near his lip. He also has a receding hairline," Ryan added informatively.

"Ryan, a lot of men could look like that."

"What are you doing? Playing devil's advocate?" he teased.

"Well, a lot of men could."

He nodded. "I know. Tomorrow I'll call Ohio and get the number of someone who belongs to their historical vehicle club. Most states have one. With luck, we'll get the name of someone who had a '56 Thunderbird."

"Then find out which of those men owned an auto dealership," Meg deduced.

Her quick thinking made him smile.

"One question," she said. "Why would he come here and use a phony name?"

"I doubt if he'd planned to. But he must have seen Elizabeth and decided to register under a phony one. No one would question it," he said easily, wheeling the car into the parking lot of a restaurant.

Briefly, Meg glanced at the pizza sign. But her interest centered on him.

He switched off the ignition. Shifting toward her, he laid an arm on the seat behind her. "If he gets desperate enough to kill her, he'd be free of any association with the auto show. He could kill her, fly or drive home to Ohio, and no one would connect him with the auto show or Elizabeth."

"I'll be." Meg gave her head a slow shake in amazement. "So when he talked to you that day and gave you the name Brey, he was already thinking about what he might have to do to Elizabeth."

Ryan slipped the key from the ignition. "That's my guess." He glanced at the clock on the dashboard. "Tomorrow we'll get some answers." In a jubilant spirit, he tossed up the car keys.

As he caught them, he leaned forward and kissed her. It was a quick kiss, a light-spirited one. It conveyed no sensuality yet seemed extremely intimate.

"Right now, why don't we celebrate over a pizza?"

"Celebrate what?"

"End of exams."

Meg laughed softly. "I'd like that." She looked toward the red-roofed building. "Pizza sounds perfect."

As they were settling into a red-vinyl booth seat a few minutes later, Ryan asked, "Pizza with everything?"

"Yes, everything." Meg frowned at the menu. "But no anchovies."

"Okay."

"And no onion. And no pepperoni."

"Anything else?"

"No."

Ryan stifled a grin over what she considered a pizza with everything on it. He placed the order for a half and half, a beer for himself, and a soda for Meg. She appeared more relaxed than usual with him. One step at a time, he reminded himself. But lately he'd begun to wonder if there would be a right moment for them. Though doubts plagued him about that, he had none about her. She was what he wanted. And he was the one that she didn't want. All because he was a cop. All because Kevin Duran had been killed while on duty. If she knew the truth about his death, would she feel differently? Perhaps, Ryan mused, but he couldn't be the one to tell her. That wasn't the solution to his problem. He looked away, knowing she had to battle her private dragon.

As Meg set the paper menu into the menu holder, her eyes fell on the gold wristwatch he wore. "Your father's?" she asked, brushing a finger across the face of the watch.

"Yeah." He looked up, and the gaze that met hers was filled with pride. "He received a medal of merit for his actions in a hostage-barricade situation. He was killed on duty during another assignment."

A fleeting quick twinge tugged at Meg's heart. "Oh, Ryan. Here I've gone on about the dangers of the job, and you . . . How old were you?"

"Twelve. It was tough for a while. My mother struggled to raise the three of us."

Meg stared down as the waitress set their drinks and the pizza on the table. When the woman walked away, Meg met his eyes again. "After having that happen, didn't your mom object to your wanting to be a cop?"

Ryan reached across the table and placed his hand on top of hers. "Meg, I had a grandmother who had a few favorite sayings, too."

Despite the previous seriousness between them, his words made her smile. Meg slipped her hand out from under his and carefully lifted a slice of pizza onto her plate. "And what was her favorite saying?"

"Don't paint the devil on the wall. She always believed you shouldn't look for trouble that isn't there." Though he grinned as he spoke, humor wasn't the mood taking hold in him. Light from the stubby candle in the red glass candleholder danced shadows across her cheek. Nearby, someone dropped coins into the jukebox. A soft melody drifted through the air and made him want to dance with her.

Meg couldn't meet the softness in his eyes. While they ate the pizza, a subtle, seductive mood lingered around them. Whether it was real or imaginary seemed unimportant. It existed, ready to make a claim on her if she allowed their eyes to meet or their hands to touch again. So she avoided contact, dodged the mood. "Why did you become a cop? Because your dad was one?"

He gave her a brief smile. "You should know. You went to the police academy because you come from the same sort of family. It's hard not to think cops and robbers when your whole life revolves around a man who thought that being a cop was the greatest job in the world."

Meg nodded understandably. Her father had said the same words himself.

"After my dad died, friends of his from the precinct kept coming around, checking on us, making sure we were okay. Policemen have always been a part of my life. And when my mom remarried—a cop," he added with a smile, "I'd already decided I was going to be one."

Meg dabbed a napkin at her lips. "And never wanted to be anything else?"

He narrowed his eyes in a thoughtful manner. "Maybe a high-priced private eye."

Meg laughed. "Like Jim?"

"Exactly."

Meg shared his amusement. "I'm sure he sees himself driving around in a Ferrari and earning a couple of hundred dollars a day. But he'd have to expand his business first, and sometimes he can't keep up with the work he has."

"Maybe he needs a partner."

"Like you?"

"Think I should?" He asked it lightly but wondered if, instead of teasing her, he should tell her that he was seriously considering quitting the force.

Meg looked down, suddenly not amused by his teasing. More than anything, she wished he would quit. Aware of his skill at reading expressions, she kept her eyes on her pizza. "This is good," she said, taking another bite.

Ryan suddenly grinned more widely. "Uh-huh."

As his gaze slid to the nearly empty pizza pan, hers followed. The only slices left were on her half. Meg sent him a sheepish smile. "I guess I like anchovies, onions and pepperoni more than I thought I did."

"Could be you like a lot of things you didn't think you'd like."

She liked him. Mentally Meg scoffed at herself. "Like" was a mild description of what she felt, she realized as she stood on the back porch and waited while he unlocked the door. She skirted naming the emotion, but had to admit that from their first meeting Ryan had sparked a sensual nerve in her.

She started to move closer to him, then heard the click of the lock. It resounded in the air like a wailing siren— a warning. Quickly, Meg stepped into the house, but instead of a fast good-night, she held the door open and faced him. She couldn't let him go. Not yet. "Want a cup of coffee?"

A smile gently played at the corners of his lips as he stepped forward into the house. "No. But..." His arm slipped around her waist and pulled her close. "I want this."

The touch of his lips on hers came as no surprise. Meg faced the seesawing emotions rampaging through her. She'd stalled at the door—deliberately. She'd offered coffee—deliberately. She wanted his kiss. She wanted more, she thought, coiling her arms around his neck. Though she felt no urgency, no demand in his kiss, it took her breath away. Slow, savoring, thorough, his mouth moved over hers until her lips parted. Tongues met, desire flared instantly. In a slow, almost cautious movement, he pulled her softness against him. Meg began to drown in sensations. Her body felt weightless, her head light. She trembled as his fingers lightly lifted her jacket from her body, and his hand slipped beneath her sweater. Gentle fingers cupped her breast, wielding a power with their tenderness. An awareness of flesh took over. Thinking became secondary to her. Touching, feeling, tasting. They mattered. They controlled her and kindled a longing she'd struggled to suppress for weeks. Even senses muddled together. Blending, they all focused on the responses slithering through her body as his hand coursed downward. It caressed her hipbone, curled over it for a second, then returned to her waist.

As he drew back, Meg was aware they were close to taking another step. A step that would mean no turning back. She wanted to, but a deep-rooted fear controlled her actions.

Words weren't needed. She yanked her jacket together, making him realize how firmly intact her defenses were again. Frustration stormed him and mingled with anger. Love was hell, he decided in a temper, turning away.

He brushed past bushes, their leaves spraying water at his face. Still muttering a curse, he stormed down the walkway toward the guest house and stepped in a puddle. Loudly and colorfully he cursed the water seeping through his shoe and sock. The angry outburst didn't help ease his anger. But if he'd stayed one more second, he'd have yelled at her. He'd have said things to her about Kevin that he'd regret later. He'd have caused her pain. Made her cry. The last thing he wanted to do was make her cry. Damn! All he wanted to do was love her.

Chapter Ten

From backstage, Meg watched as three men performed "Danny Boy." More Irish music danced on the air for the people attending the Halloween Irishfest. In the crowded auditorium, she saw familiar faces: her family, neighbors, friends, and Ryan. Seated in the row behind her family, he occasionally leaned forward to say something to her father. Cozy, Meg thought, wondering when he had met her parents. Before this, in the hospital when they'd all visited Jim? Or had Ryan approached them minutes before and introduced himself? Either way, he'd charmed her parents. Everyone was all smiles.

Meg frowned deeper over a more immediate problem. Elliott was nowhere in sight. Briefly she wondered if he'd decided to abandon his theatrical ambitions. If he had, she wished he'd told her about it.

She glanced down at her legs encased in black stockings and reached back to discreetly tug at the costume. Black, strapless, and brief, it refused to stay in place to suit her. As she tugged at the hem of the skimpy material, the bodice lowered. Meg made a face at the overabundant swell of her breasts. The costume belonged more on a beach in the French Riviera than in a room filled with family and friends.

Her eyes glued on the backstage entrance door, she impatiently tapped the toe of her black pump. Ten minutes passed before Elliott arrived. With his usual dramatic flair, he strutted in, dressed in black tie and tails. He smiled at Meg and gestured with a grand sweep of his arm toward the oversize fish tank being wheeled in by a stagehand. "The death-defying water tank," he announced as explanation to Meg.

Worry skittered through her as she watched the stagehands position the tank to the center of the stage behind the curtain.

Elliott waltzed past her. "This trick will make me the greatest magician since Houdini."

Meg double-stepped to keep up with his exuberant strides. "You've never done a trick like this before. You don't know how to do it."

"Of course, I do," he assured her, lifting his head to a prideful tilt.

But he didn't. Soon after the show began, Elliott climbed into the airtight, water-filled tank. Within seconds, he began to struggle to escape the handcuffs on his wrists and ankles. But he was stuck, unable to free himself. And time was running out. With the curtain in place over the front of the tank, the stagehands frantically rushed to unlock the numerous locks clamping shut the lid of the tank. His air nearly gone, Elliott managed to free himself from the leg cuffs, but continued to battle with the ones binding his wrists. When the stagehands removed the lid and pulled him from the water, he gasped

for air. Shaken, he nodded agreeably to Meg's insistence
that he go to the hospital.

While an accordionist filled the gap in the program,
Meg quickly changed out of her costume and into jeans
and a cable-stitch sweater. By the time she returned from
driving Elliott home from the hospital, applause was re-
sounding in the air for the end of the program.

"Elliott's all right," Meg announced as she joined her
parents outside the auditorium. Standing nearby, Ryan
said nothing, but Meg guessed his thoughts. She had ad-
amantly insisted that Elliott's work was safer than his.
Though Meg expected an I-told-you-so look from Ryan,
she saw instead an expression of concern on his face.

"Just shaken?" he asked.

Meg nodded. "That was foolish of him." Following
her parents toward the parking lot, she slowed her pace
beside Ryan. "I seem to have been wrong about his
work," she admitted.

"Not really. But like any job, it's only dangerous when
the person doesn't show caution."

Meg nodded agreeably. "Yes. He did act foolishly."

"Some cops get killed the same way."

His words came out clipped, almost forced. Meg stared
down at her feet as a distinctive silence stretched between them. Each click of her heels seemed to emphasize the unnatural quietness. Uncomfortable with it, Meg
forced herself to ask the question on her mind. "Is that
what happened to your dad?"

Ryan's head jerked toward her. Briefly, puzzlement
creased his brow. He stared for a long moment at her before answering, "No, is that the impression I gave?"

"Sort of."

"No," he repeated. "My dad died while helping res-
cue two children from a fire. He showed caution. He

followed procedures.'' Ryan gave a simple shrug of his shoulders. ''An unexpected secondary explosion occurred.''

Meg sent him an empathetic look. ''The unexpected. I understand that. Kevin, too, was the victim of fate.''

Ryan looked away, annoyed and frustrated. Kevin. A man he'd never met was controlling his future. He drew a hard breath, a controlled one, while his gaze followed her parents weaving their way between rows of parked cars. ''I've been invited to your parents' home for dinner. Want to ride with me?''

Meg turned surprised eyes up at him. ''You have? How did you manage that?''

The sight of her smile stirred his own. He felt the heaviness within him easing away as he met her sparkling eyes. ''You're looking at me as if you think I practice hocus-pocus.''

''How did you meet my parents?''

''In Washington when they came to visit Jim. And again in the hospital. I was visiting Jim one evening when they came in. We talked, your mother knew you and I were working together, found out I was coming here tonight and invited me to dinner.''

Meg gave him a tongue-in-cheek look. ''I think you're smoother than I originally gave you credit for.''

''Probably.'' He smiled, touching the small of her back and urging her toward his car. ''You might as well drive with me.''

''Might as well.''

His casualness didn't fool her. She realized in that second that he had probably planned everything carefully, even this brief time together. As he opened the car door for her, his mouth brushed her cheek. The heat of his

breath steamed against her cold flesh with his whispered
words.

"Don't underestimate me, Meg."

Underestimate Ryan Brady? Never again, Meg decided as she sat beside him in her family's dining room.
As if he belonged, he joined in conversation with her
parents, brothers, and sisters-in-law. Oddly, rather than
annoyance, Meg felt a warm glow kindling within her as
she realized how easily they'd accept him as part of the
family. Everyone liked him. Everyone would accept him.
In a family as large and close-knit as hers was, that was
important. Only she objected to him.

"Meg?" Her brother Patrick corralled her into a corner of the living room.

As he sent a furtive glance over his shoulder to see what
his parents were doing, Meg turned a puzzled look in her
brother Brian's direction. Her frown deepened as he, too,
shot a quick look at their parents before he hurried over
to join her and Patrick.

"Has Patrick told you yet?" Brian asked.

"No, I have not."

"You're not in a courtroom now, so don't drag it out,"
Brian warned. "If you do, Mom or Dad will know we're
up to something."

Meg gave her head a confused shake. She saw Ryan
standing nearby, grinning over the scenario between her
brothers. He obviously knew what she didn't. "Why
don't one of you tell me what's going on?" she said,
touching Patrick's arm.

Brian leaned close and whispered, "We want to give
them a thirty-fifth anniversary present early."

Straightening his back to emphasize the two inches he had over Brian, Patrick frowned. "I was supposed to tell her."

Meg shook her head at the sibling rivalry that occasionally still flared between them.

"A trip to Hawaii," Patrick announced in a stiff courtroom manner.

"Oh, that's a wonderful idea." She flashed a bright smile at both of her brothers. "They'll love it. Which of you thought of that?" she asked, placing one hand on Brian's shoulder and the other hand on Patrick's.

As usual, the annoyance faded between them as quickly as it had formed.

"Jim," they admitted in unison.

"Oh," Meg said simply, holding down a giggle. "Well, it's a wonderful idea."

"What about your father?" Ryan asked, raising a questioning brow.

Meg's smile widened. In the short time he had known her father, Ryan had obviously already sensed that her father's tough facade covered a marshmallow heart. She wrinkled her nose. "He'll make complaining noises that he's too old for hula dancers, but he'll be thrilled. When?" Meg asked, turning her attention back to her brothers.

"We still have to work out the details. But we thought we'd give them the trip around Thanksgiving time."

"So, Patrick," Meg said quickly as her father wandered toward them, "you found the witness for your case?"

As Patrick muttered the right response to draw their father into conversation, Ryan pretended he and Brian had been deep in discussion about skydiving.

He fit in perfectly, Meg mused. That thought returned later in the evening as she watched him concentrating on fixing her three-year-old niece's suddenly beheaded doll.

When Meg sat beside him in the car again as he drove toward home, her thoughts kept returning to her mother's last whispered words to her before she and Ryan had left the house. "You make a nice pair, Meg."

A deep, stirring need made Meg want to admit that she thought so, too. She fought herself. She and Ryan were too different. They had different tastes in foods and music. He liked jazz. She liked rock music. He liked anchovies. She hated anchovies. He liked coffee. She hated coffee. And plants. He had a green thumb with them. If she looked at one too long, it wilted. No, they weren't right for each other. So why did he seem absolutely perfect for her? He thrilled her with a look. He gentled her mood with a word. He made her smile; he made her furious. He loved her. He'd said so. If they loved each other, all the differences in the world didn't matter. Only one thing made her hesitate. He was a cop.

"I went to the police station this morning and got an okay to use their computer."

His words snapped her attention toward him. "To check out Brey?" she asked. Before he even had a chance to nod, she continued, "What did you find out? Did you learn his real name?"

Ryan glanced away from the dark suburban road that led from her parent's home toward the city. He grinned over her barrage of questions. "Yes."

Meg sent him an exasperated look. "Yes to which question?"

"I called Ohio about the historical vehicles. Government offices were closed. But I got the name of someone who sells restored vintage cars. He knew everyone in the state who'd ever had one. Ed Crandall had that Thunderbird."

Meg inched closer on the car seat and inclined her head.

"I threw his name into the police computer."

"And?"

"He didn't even have a driving ticket much less an arrest record. But his driver's license photo was brought on the screen. Brey and Ed Crandall, Jr., are the same man."

"Did you talk to Elizabeth about him?"

"She said that she never heard of him. But that's not strange. She only knows the man's face. And this guy seems to have been working hard to make sure she doesn't see him."

"Is he a legitimate businessman?"

"He appears to be. But your graphologist told us he's a thrill seeker. A lot of affluent people commit crimes for reasons other than money. Maybe he's one of them. Regardless, he's the one to look out for tomorrow at the auto show. And the police have assigned Elizabeth protection. So we'll have help guarding her."

"I'll..."

"Watch her. That's all," Ryan said sternly. "You won't..."

Meg leaned toward him and pressed a fingertip to his lips to silence him. "I won't do anything risky or dumb. You either."

His eyes met hers in the dark interior of the car. "Meg, I make it a point not to do anything risky or dumb."

Meg gave her head a quick nod and slid back to her side of the car, bracing her back against the locked door. Their conversation had moved too close to her fears for him. She didn't want to discuss the danger in his job. She knew it existed. And nothing he said would alleviate the uncertainty that went hand in hand with that danger. "When he held up the bank, it was armed robbery wasn't it?"

"Uh-huh."

As Ryan turned the car onto the scenic drive along the lake, Meg looked at the whitecaps swirling fiercely onto the dark beach. She felt a shiver run through her. Her heart quickened as she thought about the man. He was a criminal. She closed her eyes, trying not to think about the gun involved in the bank robbery. The gun he probably wouldn't hesitate to use this time. The police department is protecting Elizabeth now, Meg reminded herself. They would handle everything. No, she realized. Ryan had taken a job to protect Elizabeth. He wouldn't shirk that duty.

The moon slipped behind a cloud, darkening the night and the lake. The dim lights of yachts docked in the harbor wavered before her eyes as raindrops began to dot the car windows. By the time Ryan turned the car into the driveway, a drizzle had begun. Meg flipped up the collar of her coat before she stepped from the car. Willingly she accepted the arm Ryan draped around her shoulder. Huddled close to him, she watched raindrops gently plop onto his nose and cheeks. Squinting against the wetness, she released a soft laugh. "You're getting the worst of this."

His lips brushed the bridge of her nose. "Isn't rainwater supposed to be good for the hair?"

Meg giggled. "Who told you that?"

"My sisters always said that. And they'd set out a bucket to catch the rain," he told her as they hurried up the stairs toward the front door.

"To wash their hair." Meg nodded agreeably. "I used to do that, too."

At her words, his eyes, then his hand, caressed the glistening raven strands. "Is that why it shines?"

"Oh, I don't do that anymore," Meg said as they reached the porch landing and she looked down to hunt through her purse for her keys. "The air is too dirty now."

While she rummaged through the zippered compartments, his fingers raked through the strands at the back of her head. The scent of lemon drifted toward him, shooting a quick, unexpected demand on his body. "It feels like silk." Even to his own ears, his voice sounded thick, huskier than usual.

Meg stilled. Without turning around, she realized how close he stood behind her. His breath had fluttered heat across her jaw and temple. His closeness swarmed in on her. Meg pushed her wallet aside and squeezed her fingers down to the bottom lining of her purse. Still no keys. "I'll find them," she assured him, the pounding of her heart racing the beat of the falling rain. "I hope you're good at waiting."

"For as long as I have to."

Meg's fingers closed over the key case and tightened as his lips gently nibbled at her earlobe. Light kisses shot a tremor through her. "Here," she said in a rush, holding up the keys. His fingers closed over hers and slipped the case from her hand. In fascination, she stared at his profile and the beads of moisture glistening on his face.

Men looked enticing wet, Meg thought not for the first time in her life. She'd spent hours of her summer vacations with high-school friends, lying on one of Chicago's beaches, basking in the sun and watching sun-browned men trudge from the lake onto the sand. Their hair wet, their flesh sleek from the water, they'd provided her and her friends with carefree summer enjoyment. But no man, not even Kevin, had stirred a deeper womanly drive in her than Ryan did.

While she clung to objectivity, both of his hands cupped her shoulders and turned her to face him. She should pull away, she told herself, but the gentle hand on her spine seemed too powerful to resist. His fingers splayed and slid around her waist, tugged her closer. Meg released a soft moan. "Ryan, you're not making this any easier."

"I know," he murmured, the heat of his breath warming the shell of her ear. In his whole life, he'd never walked so softly with any woman. But Meg wasn't just any woman to him. He wanted her—craved her kisses— longed to arouse the passion that he sensed she'd kept controlled. So easily, he could solve the problem between them. Stop being a cop. Jim and he had talked often about a partnership. But regardless of what Ryan decided, he knew he needed her to say she'd have him on any terms. The thought seemed sentimental and romantic. Ryan smiled to himself. If he wasn't that kind of man, he'd tell her he'd been considering quitting the force. Too easy, he decided. That solution seemed too easy for a man who believed love could overcome any obstacles. She had to love him enough to want him even if he was a cop. He touched her cheek with his other hand. He needed a kiss. Damn, he needed a lot more. But for the moment, a kiss. One kiss.

Malleable, yielding, she forgot about resisting. She shoved aside all the reasons why she shouldn't get involved with him, why she shouldn't make love with him, why she shouldn't love him. As his mouth sought the curve of her neck and lingered, his hands created a fiery explosion within her. Her breath quickened as his head lowered and his lips paused at the pulse in her neck before seeking the tender flesh at her collarbone. She lost the ability to stop him and leaned limply against him.

She lost. And won. Desire pounded in her as his mouth covered hers with a hard kiss. Her lips answered the greediness in his. Want overshadowed other feelings. Her hands framed his face to feel the hardness of his features, the softness of his flesh. As his tongue slipped between her lips, her lashes flickered, and her arms coiled around his neck, pulling his face closer to hers. For a few seconds she wanted not to think too rationally. Just for a few seconds. She saw no harm in a few short, frivolous seconds of allowing her emotions to lead her. No harm, she reminded herself as she began to feel a floaty weakness flooding over her. She knew her feet touched the ground, but she lost all contact with her own body. She felt his. Its hardness and its heat. His mouth demanded yet was disturbingly gentle, persuasive as he deepened the kiss, snatching her breath from her. Still, she didn't stop him.

She felt a stirring, a longing to touch and examine his face in the way that a blind person courses a trail over features to see them. She felt the hardness of his cheekbones, the soft flesh of his cheek, the rough stubble of his masculine beard. She savored the texture beneath her fingertips as her hand explored the thickness of hair at the nape of his neck, felt the moisture of a misty rain on his flesh.

She clung harder, wanting to hold him near far longer than she dared. One more second and she knew she'd have no will of her own to stop. She took a step back, halting when the back of her legs touched the door.

Ryan drew a harsh breath. "How long do you think you can deny what we both . . . ?"

She looked away, realizing she'd underestimated her own feelings for him. Those few seconds had played havoc with her resolve. She felt an ache beginning to build slowly within her as she gave a fleeting thought to never letting him hold her again. She wanted his closeness, his kisses. She wanted him. Reasoning and logic never would override the emotion that stirred for him.

Ryan watched fear cloud her eyes. He'd felt her surrender. If he drew her close again, he knew she'd never resist—at least, not now. Later, she'd be furious, hate herself for the weakness, maybe hate him for arousing it within her. Her harsh breaths matched his. And he saw desire, but he also saw confusion. He wanted her more than he'd ever wanted any woman. But first he wanted her to admit that she loved him. For both their sakes, she had to say it. He watched a storm brew in her eyes. Angry thoughts straightened her back and pride raised her chin. He didn't want to steal that trait from her, but he needed one last kiss. He needed to remind her what she was running from. Briefly his lips touched hers.

Meg had no defense. They both knew now what the problem was. She loved him and didn't want to.

"You can't run from this, Meg," he said softly as she turned the doorknob and swung open the door.

She heard frustration in his voice and a hint of anger. It stilled her in the doorway. For a second, the cold chill of winter seemed more pronounced. Unconsciously, she shivered. "I won't let it happen," she insisted, keeping her back to him.

"Too late, Meg. It already has happened," Ryan assured her before she closed the door behind her.

Chapter Eleven

Morning sunlight glared through the front window of the car. Ryan squinted against the brightness as he watched Meg descend the front-porch stairs. For a brief moment, he wondered which of them was more stubborn. As she drew closer, he decided that he was. He had too much to lose if he gave up.

He'd tried to make sense of his recent actions. An incurable romantic, he saw his unwavering pursuit of her as the only option. But the analytical, practical side of him that had made him succeed and gain promotions in police work viewed his single-mindedness about Meg as downright foolish. Yet "foolish" and "in love" seemed an accurate description of him ever since they'd met. He'd never had any other woman haunt his mind as she did. Everything about her pleased him. He wanted to hear her laugh, see her smile, know her touch for the rest of his life. Somehow he would. In the past, patience had worked well in ferreting out crooks and capturing them.

They challenged him. And so did Meg. She was probably the biggest challenge he'd ever had in his life, he thought as she opened the car door and slid in. But some challenges were worth extra effort.

Though anxious and uncertain what his mood would be like after the previous night, Meg began to relax during the ride toward the auto show. "I talked to Jim this morning," she told him. "He's anxious to get home."

Ryan shot a quick grin at her. "He told me he's counting the hours until tomorrow."

"He doesn't like being cooped up."

"He doesn't like Nurse Magoo."

Meg laughed. "That's true. If she looked like a fashion model, he'd be moaning that they were releasing him too soon." At Ryan's agreeing nod, Meg gave vent to a question that had plagued her for days. "Will you stay for a while? He'll be in a leg cast."

Ryan looked askance at her. "I'm staying."

"That's good." Though she tried to keep emotion out of her voice, she watched a smile tug at the corners of his mouth. Did he hear the joy in her voice that he was staying longer? Meg silently moaned, wishing she could come to terms with his job. Everything would be perfect then. But no matter how much she tried, no matter how much she loved him, she couldn't hurdle that obstacle between them. Though she no longer grieved for Kevin, if he hadn't been a cop, she knew he'd be alive now. That thought constantly returned whenever she even considered a life with Ryan. At any time, he could be taken from her, too.

As he stopped the car and reached to the backseat for his heavy jacket, his sports jacket billowed. Meg saw his shoulder holster and his gun. No, she knew she'd never overcome that obstacle about the uncertainty in his job.

No matter how good a cop he was, because of Kevin she'd learned that good cops weren't free from the uncertainty or the danger.

When Jim came home tomorrow, she'd stop working at the office. She might even take a short trip, visit a friend in Milwaukee. Whatever she did, she'd put some distance between her and Ryan.

A large crowd jammed the showrooms filled with vintage cars. Beneath the spotlights, their chrome glistened and their highly polished bodies shone, dazzling the eye. Beside each car stood a beautiful woman to complete any male's fantasy about how the purchase of such a car might change his life.

Ryan, too, Meg thought whimsically. When they'd first entered the building, he'd stalled before a meticulous-looking 1926 Model T Ford. With a look of respectful awe, he'd inspected the vintage automobile. It gleamed as if it were this year's new model. While Ryan continued to admire the car's polished chrome bumpers and stainless-steel hoses, Meg scanned the crowd but saw nothing threatening. Dressed in a flowing white chiffon gown, Elizabeth stood beside a deep burgundy automobile and explained the features of the 1929 Mercedes Benz.

"Meg Gallagher, is that you?"

Meg stilled instantly. Her smile sprang quickly to her face as she recognized the gray-haired man with the walrus mustache. Wearing a security guard's uniform, the man was an ex-policeman who'd worked with her father. "Mr. Tillman. How are you?"

"I'm fine. Last time we talked, you were wearing braces and telling your father that the man down the street was running a counterfeiting ring."

Meg laughed. "I had an overactive imagination."

"As I recall, you did," he said in an affectionate, teasing voice. "But good instincts. Didn't your father check the man out and find out he'd committed some burglaries in the neighborhood?"

Though Meg tried not to, she beamed. "Yes, he did."

"You told me that day that you were going to be a police chief someday. Did you go into law enforcement?"

"I'm studying to be a government investigator."

"That's good. I bet your father's proud."

"I think so," she answered, letting her eyes roam away for a second. Smiling, Elizabeth was answering a teenage boy's question about the automobile's engine. As he asked another question, obviously more interested in her than the car, she held onto a polite smile. Seeing nothing unusual, Meg returned her attention to the gray-haired man beside her. "You should call Dad. He'd like to see you."

"I'll have to do that. I'd like to see him, too. I haven't seen him since I retired." A sadness dulled his eyes. "Guess I'll always miss being on the force."

Meg offered an understanding smile as she remembered he'd been forced to retire after a heart attack. "My dad said it's hard to stop being a cop."

"It's more than that." He looked out at the crowd with unseeing eyes. "I never finished my last assignment. We were moving in on a big drug deal last October, and the case was muffed. Right after that I had my heart attack. It took my partner another year to get enough new evidence to convict those dealers."

Meg frowned over his words. "In October?" At his nod, she questioned further. "A year ago in October?"

"That's right. Right before Halloween."

Her mind raced back. She remembered he'd been at the station house on the night Kevin had died. Though a sadness had settled over the room because a cop had been killed, she remembered now that Tillman had said something about his assignment being bungled by an overzealous rookie. That evening she'd been too numb to think about anything except that Kevin was dead. She hadn't paid a lot of attention to Tillman then. Grief-stricken, she'd listened to Kevin's captain confirm that he was the cop who had been killed. Her mind had refused all other thoughts then.

"I'll always wish that I'd finished my last assignment," Tillman said wistfully, snapping Meg's attention back to him.

He obviously hadn't been any more aware of her that evening than she'd been of him. Kevin and she hadn't been officially engaged. There was no reason for Tillman to have noticed her in the police station. And Meg realized he didn't understand that he was discussing something very important to her. "A drug deal?" she questioned, her mind suddenly stormed by a dozen unanswered questions.

At his nod, Meg looked away, certain she'd paled as suspicions began to take root in her mind. With her peripheral vision, she saw Elizabeth leaving the platform. Meg watched her head toward the washrooms at the back of the showroom. A man skirted around a crowd of people and took the same path that she did. A tall, thin man with a receding hairline.

Meg's eyes darted toward Ryan. He'd seen Ed Brey, too. Glancing back, Elizabeth stilled for a second. Her eyes flew wide as she saw the man. Ryan was already heading toward her, but Elizabeth turned and ran toward the exit.

Meg took off, not even excusing herself as she rushed toward Ryan.

He shouted at her, pointing his arm at the policeman, "Alert him."

Panic swelled up in her. "Ryan?"

"Go!" His gaze clung to Brey racing his way around the back of the showroom. Then for a brief second he glanced at her. He saw fear in her eyes, felt stunned by it. "Meg, go!" he ordered.

She wanted to scream, to cling. But knew she couldn't. He was a cop. He faced the danger of that job willingly. Meg knew that nothing she said would stop him. And he was careful. He'd told her that he was, she reminded herself, whirling away to obey his order.

While Ryan pushed his way through the crowd, she ran across the room toward the policeman stationed near Elizabeth's platform. Meg rushed the words on one breath. "The man is after Elizabeth."

As the policeman raced across the showroom toward the exit, Meg followed, not allowing herself time to think. At the exit Tillman joined the pursuit. Stepping outside, Meg nearly plowed into Tillman's back when he stopped abruptly. Over his shoulder, Meg saw Ed Brey, his hands against the wall. Ryan stood on one side of him while the policeman frisked and then handcuffed the thin man.

Looking like a fawn frozen by blinding headlights, Elizabeth had plastered herself against the building.

On the ground near her was Brey's gun.

Meg watched Ryan move beside her. He spoke in soothing tones. He was a good cop, Meg realized, admiring his manner of dealing with a victim.

Though his eyes briefly met Meg's, he seemed to avoid longer visual contact with her. He slipped a hand around Elizabeth's arm. Urging her toward the doorway, he finally looked at Meg. "I have to take Elizabeth to the station. I'll see you later."

Meg said nothing. She knew he wanted her to nod agreeably. His brows knitted, and for a second she saw something flash in his eyes. She couldn't decipher the emotion. Questions nagged at her mind, confused her. Commotion to her right swerved her attention away from him. As police ushered Brey past curious spectators, Meg's gaze settled on the security guard, Tom Tillman. She needed to talk to him. At the moment she needed answers to questions. "Later," Meg assured, looking back at Ryan, but he'd already moved away. His hand still firm under Elizabeth's arm, he shielded her from the crowd as they made their way toward his car.

Meg's questions were brief, on target. Because she was blunt with Tom Tillman, all he had to do was verify what Meg had begun to suspect. Within fifteen minutes, she was driving her car toward the hospital to talk to her brother.

Meg stood a foot away from Jim and watched her brother hand-lift his leg and swivel himself to the edge of the bed to a sitting position.

"Jim, tell me the truth," she insisted.

He fidgeted uncomfortably and stared at his bare feet. "Meg, no one meant to hurt you. We tried to protect you."

Meg drew a deep breath, determined to stay calm. All her life she'd heard her family speak those same words. "From what?"

He kept looking down, not meeting her eyes. He hadn't met them since she'd walked into the room and demanded to know the truth about Kevin's death. An unnatural frown deeply creased deep lines across Jim's forehead. "You believed Kevin was...was perfect. Since he was dead, no one saw any reason to take that from you. And you wanted to get away," he added quickly. "Because you went to California for a few weeks, the follow-up stories in the newspapers, the media's questions never reached you. Everyone thought we'd only make you feel worse if we told you the truth."

Meg sank slowly to the chair near his bed. "Kevin responded to a domestic quarrel, didn't he?"

"He did. But the apartment building had a known drug dealer. The investigative department was closing in on him. Everyone at the department knew that, including Kevin. But he wanted to make a name for himself. Without authorization, he went to the man's apartment. He walked in on a drug deal. The only problem was the dealer had a partner in another room. Kevin was shot in the back." Jim inched his hips forward on the mattress and reached out for her hand. "Meg, he had no business there. He showed no caution and he didn't radio in that he was going there. He didn't follow procedures and ask for a backup."

Her eyes shot up. "Why didn't he?"

"Because he knew he'd be told not to go there."

Meg nodded, but because she'd loved Kevin, something inside her refused to be disloyal to him, to believe he'd deliberately done wrong. "He was ambitious," she said in his defense.

Jim sent her a sad look. "He was overzealous," he corrected. "He balked at discipline and procedures. He did that night, too. Because he wanted to make the bust. He wanted to be the hero." His voice softened to a whisper. "He got killed, Meg, because he didn't follow his training. He took an unnecessary chance, a dumb chance that cost him his life. He also blew the investigation. If he hadn't been shot . . ."

At his silence, she raised her head slowly, sensing the words he was having difficulty saying. "Go on," she urged softly.

"He would have been kicked off the force."

"Why did you all keep this from me?"

"We didn't intend to. Some of it came out in the newspapers, but you were gone. When you came back from California, you had accepted his death. We didn't know how to tell you the truth. No one wanted to hurt you. And . . . and . . ." Jim shook his head. "Damn, but we all knew we'd made a mistake, especially after Ryan came. We saw what was happening between you two and realized that if you'd known the truth things would have been different between you two. The job turned danger-ous for Kevin because he acted foolishly."

A numbness weighed her down. Meg felt empty. She'd been resisting Ryan because of a fear aroused by Kevin's death. He wasn't the cop she'd thought he'd been. He wasn't anything like her father had been. He wasn't any-thing like Ryan.

Jim sent her a regretful look. "I'm sorry," he said softly. "I really am. We love you. That's our only ex-cuse."

Meg nodded and offered a weak smile. "I know. I'm partly to blame. I did think he was a perfect cop. I saw him as ambitious, but I didn't see him clearly. I didn't see his disregard for rules. I knew he was impatient and im-petuous, but I never thought he'd show those qualities while working. I understand," she assured him and leaned forward, accepting his embrace. "I really do un-derstand."

His hands cupped her shoulders and drew her back to see her face. "Now what?"

"I have to talk to Ryan."

The first snowfall of the season began as Meg sped home. Soft, fluttering flakes danced in the air, slowing a normally creeping rush-hour traffic. Time ticked by. Valuable time, she thought, mulling over and regretting her unresponsiveness to Ryan before he'd left with Elizabeth. But wanting answers about Kevin had preoccupied her. Worry weighed her down now. What had Ryan thought? She smothered doubts as quickly as they formed. She had made a decision now. He'd wanted her before, hadn't he? Why wouldn't he want her now? she reminded herself. Still, uncertainty mingled with her impatience during the time-consuming drive home.

Certain he'd finished at the police station, Meg hurried down the walkway toward the guest house. Snow dusted the ground with a patchy carpet of white, shivered her with cold. Uneasiness stormed her as she stood before the door. If he were home, she'd hear the radio. He liked music on all the time. Meg smiled wryly, wondering when she'd begun to notice little things about him. From the moment they'd met, she realized. She gave her head a slight shake, wishing she hadn't been so blind, so stubborn.

She rapped harder on the door. Still no answer. Meg glanced at the kitchen window. In that second hysteria flashed through her. The philodendron was gone from the windowsill. Time again became paramount in her mind. Quickly she dug into her purse for the master key. As she opened the door, a knot bunched in her stomach.

Everything he owned was gone. Minus his possessions, the guest house looked barren. For a long moment, Meg stood in the middle of the living room. An emptiness drifted over her. She felt lost, alone. The urge to cry stirred a lump in her throat, but she swallowed hard against the constriction. Tears never helped ease the pain of a loss. And that's what she felt. A grieving. Why? she wondered accusingly. Why had she been so stubborn to see the truth, to realize that Ryan wasn't like Kevin. Why hadn't she recognized that she'd been running from the very pain she was feeling now? Loss. She hadn't wanted to love Ryan for fear of losing him. So she'd fought emotions, had never allowed herself that love but had lost anyway. God, what a fool she was. All because she was afraid. Since Kevin's death, she'd allowed fear to control her life. She'd made the decision to keep herself free from risks. But love was always a risk of sorts. That was what she'd forgotten. There was always a chance the heart might break, but that was a risk that had to be taken. If she refused to take that risk, she'd lose. Had lost, she realized, looking again around the empty room.

One plant remained. In the middle of the white Formica kitchen table sat the African violets. He'd said they were a challenge. Yet he'd left them. Had he thought they were too much of a challenge to bother with? Had he decided she was, too?

Meg swallowed hard again and moved closer to the folded paper lying on the table in front of the plant. She reached for the paper, then pulled her hand back as if it were burned. Fear of a different sort coursed through her. She wrestled with the idea of a goodbye note. As she unfolded the paper, her worst fear became a reality.

Meg
Take care of this one for me. It couldn't take the move. Too delicate to risk such a change.

                                                          Ryan

Meg drew a long hard breath, holding back a sob as anger flashed through her. He'd said he'd stay. He'd promised he'd help Jim for a while longer. Fighting to stay calm helped. She was certain he hadn't left town yet. He'd go see Jim first. He'd go to the office. There was paperwork to finish. He'd be at the office, Meg thought in a rational moment. It might not be too late.

The ten-minute drive from the house to the office seemed like a matter of hours. And what if he's not there? Meg wondered. What would she do then?

By the time the elevator reached the floor of the office, she'd made a decision. She'd go to New Mexico. Tenacity didn't belong only to him. She had plenty of that same trait.

Meg saw the light through the frosted glass of the office door. Her steps faltered as she released a long breath. Not too late. Now, she thought, trying to gather her thoughts into some coherent order to make sense. But she kept seeing the look in his eyes when she hadn't answered him. Disappointment, frustration, pain. What if he didn't care anymore that she loved him? That she wanted what he'd wanted?

Before she had time to consider a rejection, she pushed at the office door.

His head bent, he hunched over Jim's desk. Writing, he didn't notice her. Was he making the last entry on the report in the Elizabeth Howard case? Meg wondered. She'd expected him to take time to do that. He was a thorough man, who'd revealed he didn't do things halfheartedly.

Feeling calmed by the sight of him, Meg took a step forward. Then she saw the canvas bag sitting on the floor next to the desk. He was leaving? Proof existed before her eyes. For a few moments during the drive she'd tried to delude herself, had prayed that she'd misconstrued his note. Now she knew she hadn't. Worry, unsureness and a trace of cowardliness rippled through her. Meg fought all the feelings and cleared her throat to get his attention.

As his head snapped up, butterflies flittered in her stomach. "You're working late."

He leaned back on the chair. Though his eyes met hers, they held none of their usual teasing sparkle. "I wanted to finish up the file on Elizabeth."

Meg gave an understanding nod. "What . . . what happened at the station?" she asked, forcing herself to step further into the room.

"Brey admitted everything. Five years ago, he was just the spoiled son of a rich man. He and a few buddies of his decided to rob the bank—for thrills."

"Oh," she said on a weak tone, moving closer to the desk. "So the case is closed?"

"For us it is. Except you might have to testify at the trial."

He kept studying her, making her nervous. He'd looked at her in a similar fashion the first time they'd met. Only this time they'd reversed positions. The thought stirred a small, nervous smile at the corners of her lips.

A frown entered his eyes. "What's so amusing?"

"The first time we met you were standing here—where I am now."

"And you were holding a gun on me. Confidently, I might add."

Meg released a soft, uncertain laugh. "Things have changed a lot since then."

His brief, reminiscing smile faded. "Have they?"

"I have. I've changed." He kept staring at her, saying nothing. The ticking of the desk clock filled the room with sound. Her eyes shifted to it. "I suppose you haven't a lot of time?"

Ryan inclined his head in puzzlement. Time was something he had a lot of. Especially too much time without her. As she began pacing in front of his desk, amusement mingled in with his confusion over her remark. "Meg, sit down, will you?"

"I can't." She charged to the window and stared at the view of a red brick wall. Snow flurries waltzed past the window. "I don't know where to begin." Keeping her back to him, she struggled to think coherently. "I told you right from the start that I wasn't interested in involvement with a cop. You knew that," she added, not waiting for his response. "And you knew why I felt that way. Fear. But until today, I didn't realize I was putting myself through a different kind of agony." She heard him release a long breath, and then heard the chair squeak as he stood up. Meg kept staring out the window. Kept talking. "I know now you're not the same kind of policeman that Kevin was. I learned that on the night he was killed he didn't do as he'd been trained to do. Jim told me that he doubted Kevin would have kept his job for long. You're not like him at all. That's what I've been blind to."

Ryan felt his heart leap. He wanted to yank her into his arms, but, warily, he kept himself from jumping to conclusions. "As a motorcycle cop, he had a different kind of job."

The unnatural hesitancy in his voice swirled her around. "That's not what I mean. He was impulsive, impatient. He hated waiting for anything. You're just the opposite. You know how to wait, you're willing to show caution. You wouldn't have been promoted so often if you weren't an excellent cop, one who understands the importance of following procedures.'' Meg paused for a second. "You knew about Kevin, didn't you?"

Ryan nodded, wondering if she'd understand why he hadn't said anything. He stared at her shoulder and the dots of snow sprinkled on her jacket. He wanted to touch her, make contact, brush the flakes away.

His eyes shifted away from the damp cloth. "I wasn't the right one to do it."

She watched concern cloud his eyes. In his own gentle way, he'd tried to tell her. "You did try, didn't you? On the night Elliott's escape trick failed, you said that any job was dangerous when the person didn't show caution. At first I thought you were talking about Elliott, but then because you were so quiet, I thought you were discussing your father."

He nodded. "I remember. You asked about him. I wanted to tell you what I knew about Kevin." He shrugged a shoulder. "I couldn't, Meg. You'd have run."

The statement was such a simple one, yet truer than Meg wanted to admit. If he had told her the truth about Kevin's death, she might have thought he was trying to ruin the memories she had with Kevin. How blind she'd been to so much truth, she realized. Ryan shifted his weight from one foot to the other. As he imperceptibly moved to turn away, panic filled Meg that she wouldn't get a chance to tell him what she really felt. "Ryan, don't go."

His head swung back. For a long moment, he narrowed his eyes at her and studied her expression, trying to decipher the emotion behind her words.

"I know I've acted foolish, hardheaded, difficult and..." His silence continued. Frustrated and apprehensive, Meg added, "You can stop me whenever you think I've said enough to convince you."

"Convince me of what?"

"That I love you." She straightened her shoulders. "I've never done this before."

"Done what?"

Color brightened her cheeks. "Proposed."

He sent her a disbelieving look. "Proposed? Like marriage?" At her nod he smiled and moved closer. "Well, I've never done it before, either. But why don't you let me give it a try first?" he said, resting his hand on her hipbone.

Joy mingled with relief, relaxing her. Relaxing seemed a peculiar thing to do while her heart pounded in a wild, erratic beat.

"I can't give you guarantees, Meg, on how much time we'll have together. But whether it's a short time or fifty years, I'll make them the best years you've ever had."

Meg slid her arms around his neck. "I know now that not being with you is more painful than anything else ever could be." She felt like giggling as he tugged her closer. "And I thought I wouldn't find you before you left. I didn't know what I was going to do with that...that plant."

"The African violet?"

"Yes. When I saw your note..."

His head reared back. "Meg, wait a minute. Did you think I was leaving town?"

Her eyes shot over his shoulder to his canvas bag. "What do you call that? People pack them when they're going on trips—or going home."

"Meg, your brother is coming home today. I moved out of the guest house and rented an apartment near here."

"Then why did you leave the plant?"

"African violets don't adapt well to different environments. I didn't want to risk moving it. The rest of the plants are jammed inside my car."

"You mean you aren't leaving? You never planned to leave? You..." Meg made a face. "I should clobber you. I thought I was never going to see you again."

He laughed and tightened his hold on her. "I told you that I'm a patient man. Even if it took a long time for you to admit you loved me, I planned on waiting."

Meg framed his face with her hands. "I love you. And I'll do my best not to kill your plants."

He rocked a hand in a maybe gesture. "I'll *try* to eat breakfast."

"Sounds like we might do all right," she teased.

"I knew that long ago."

"You did?"

"Definitely. Love at first sight." Laughing over the astonished look in her eyes, he placed a finger under her chin to close her mouth.

"I thought you were kidding when you said that." She beamed. "First time you saw me in the office?" she asked, prodding, suddenly enjoying the idea.

"Long before that. Years ago."

"Years ago?"

"That's right. Years ago Jim showed me your photograph. I came here hoping to find out if I loved only a photograph. Right from the start you had me. I stared at that gun in your hands and decided life never would be dull with you. And never have I wanted anyone like I want you. I knew I would never give up until you'd say you'd marry me."

Shock settled on her face. "You really meant it when you said that you believed in love at first sight."

His lips brushed the tip of her nose. "With you. Now, will you marry me?"

"Yes, I want to marry you," she said, brushing strands of hair away from his forehead.

He grabbed her hand and pressed his lips against her knuckles. "That was amazingly simple."

"You asked the right question." Teasingly she kissed a corner of his mouth. "Tell me about New Mexico."

"Why?"

"I want to know something about the place if I'm going to live there."

"You are?"

Meg narrowed her eyes curiously. "Married people usually live together."

"We will. Here."

"You transferred here?" she asked. Having to live in New Mexico had seemed inevitable to her. "But you'll lose your sergeant's rank, won't you?"

"I expected to."

A concerned look clouded her eyes. "Ryan, do you want to do that?"

"Definitely. I'm leaving the police force. Jim and I talked months ago about a partnership. That—" he paused "—and you were two of the reasons why I came here."

Even though she had come to accept his work as a policeman, relief flooded her. "*When* did you decide this?"

"Before I came here, I'd given it a lot of thought. But I wanted to see the city, get used to everything before I made a firm decision."

Meg gave his arm an ineffectual punch. "Why didn't you tell me?"

"I did—sort of," he admitted with a grin.

Meg searched her mind. A memory flashed back to her. He had said something about a partnership, but she'd believed he was teasing when he'd said he'd considered being a high-priced private eye. "You didn't say it seriously."

"I wanted to tell you that I was serious, but if I'd told you, I wouldn't have known that you'd love me on any terms."

A knowing smile tugged a corner of her lips. "So you need certainty in your life, too."

"Uh-huh," he murmured, pressing his lips against the curve of her neck.

Meg snuggled closer to him. "We're quite a pair."

"Perfect," he added before pressing his mouth against hers.

FREE!

Never Before Published

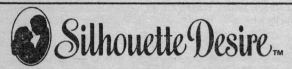

Silhouette Desire™

by

Stephanie James!

This title *Saxon's Lady* will be available exclusively through this offer. This book will not be sold through retail stores.

A year ago she left for the city. Now he's come to claim her back. Read about it in *Saxon's Lady*, a sensual, romantic story of the same excellent quality as the over two dozen other Silhouette romances written by Stephanie James.

To participate in this exciting offer, collect three proof-of-purchase coupons from the back pages of July and August Desire titles. Mail in the three coupons plus $1.00 for postage and handling ($1.25 in Canada) to reserve your copy of this unique book. This special offer expires October 31st, 1987.

Look for details in July & August Silhouette Desire titles!

Doff-A-1

COMING NEXT MONTH

#514—THE THINGS WE DO FOR LOVE—Glenda Sands
When pretty Shelby Thurston offered Austin Hastings ready employment, he
was intrigued enough to accept. Little did the handsome engineer know the
talents the job entailed. But he would do anything for love—and Shelby.

#515—TO CHOOSE A WIFE—Phyllis Halldorson
Susan Alessandro was a blond angel, but Marco Donatello had never been
attracted to innocent romantics, especially one his father had handpicked for
him to marry. They had nothing in common—except their growing love for
each other.

#516—A DANGEROUS PROPOSITION—Melodie Adams
As an undercover investigator, Blake Marlow was a professional. So why was
suspected smuggler Cassandra Wyatt giving him sleepless nights? He should
have been able to handle a routine case, but his unexpected feelings for
Cassandra were anything but routine.

#517—MAGGIE MINE—Karen Young
Maggie Taylor believed in love, marriage and happily ever after.
Cash McKenzie was a dyed-in-the-wool cynic, disillusioned with romance.
Could Maggie reawaken the romantic in Cash and teach him to love again?

#518—THE BOY NEXT DOOR—Arlene James
Ronni Champlain still cringed at the memory of her adolescent crush on
Jeff Paul Logan, and she was determined to stay away from him. But when her
little sister started to gaze at him with hero-worship in her eyes, Ronni knew she
had to step in. Could she save her sister, or would Ronni soon fall back under
Jeff Paul's magical spell?

#519—MR. LONELYHEARTS—Suzanne Forster
When Scott "The Hunter" Robinson refused to notice Amy Dwyer, she wrote
to her paper's advice column for help. She was surprised to find that Hunter
was the new columnist! Soon, Amy was following his advice—right into
his heart.

AVAILABLE THIS MONTH: